Earthquake-Tsunami-
Disaster in Japan 2011

Frank Senauth

authorHOUSE®

AuthorHouse™
1663 Liberty Drive
Bloomington, IN 47403
www.authorhouse.com
Phone: 1-800-839-8640

© 2011 Frank Senauth. All rights reserved

No part of this book may be reproduced, stored in a retrieval system, or transmitted by any means without the written permission of the author.

First published by AuthorHouse   12/7/2011

ISBN: 978-1-4670-4166-9 (sc)
ISBN: 978-1-4670-4165-2 (hc)
ISBN: 978-1-4670-4164-5 (e)

Library of Congress Control Number: 2011917607

Printed in the United States of America

Any people depicted in stock imagery provided by Thinkstock are models, and such images are being used for illustrative purposes only.
Certain stock imagery © Thinkstock.

This book is printed on acid-free paper.

Because of the dynamic nature of the Internet, any web addresses or links contained in this book may have changed since publication and may no longer be valid. The views expressed in this work are solely those of the author and do not necessarily reflect the views of the publisher, and the publisher hereby disclaims any responsibility for them.

OTHER BOOKS BY FRANK SENAUTH

Published by Minarva Publishing in the United Kingdom
A Wish to Die – A Will to Live
A Time to Live – A Time to Die
To Save Flight 608 from Disaster

Published by Dorrance Publishing in the United States
To Save the Titanic from Disaster – Part One

Published by Trafford Publishing in Victoria, Canada
To Save the Titanic from Disaster – Part Two
A Cry for Help (The Fantastic Adventures of Elian Gonzalez)
"A Wish to Die – A Will to Live
A Day of Terror (Events of the 11th of September 2001)
The Command (Events of the War in Iraq)
Cold Days pf the Snipers (Events of the two black snipers in the United States)

Published by Outskirts Press in the United States
Tsunami 2004 (The worst storm to hit Asia)
A Morning of Terror (Events of the bombing in London, England)
Hurricane Katrina (The worst storm to hit the Gulf – Part One)
Hurricane Katrina (The worst storm to hit the Gulf – Part Two)
A Month of Terror (The war between the Israelis and the Hezbollah)
The Collapse of the 1-35 Mississippi River Bridge

Published by AuthorHouse in the United States
The Last Call (Curse of the Bhutto's Name)
The Making of Guyana
Massacre of Mumbai
Day of the Dinosaur
The Making of a President
The Making of Trinidad and Tobago
The Making and the Destruction of Haiti
The Making of Jamaica.

AUTHOR'S NOTE

    I didn't know too much about the Japanese people but after watching the incredible scenes on CNN, I felt really sad for all those wonderful people who suffered tremendously from the earthquake and tsunami in Japan. The great tsunami had taken all of the towns and its people and belongings. The people of Japan had a fight on their hands and no one to help them, but they are strong people and they will survive in the midst of a rough time. They are a proud people and no one can take that away from them.

A SPECIAL DEDICATION TO THE JAPANESE PEOPLE

I hereby dedicate this book to all the wonderful people of Japan whose dreams never came true because of the earthquake and tsunami in Japan on March 11, 2011, which has taken their dreams away. They are strong and they will find a way to come back to reality. God bless them all.

Earthquake–Tsunami–Disaster in Japan 2011

THE HISTORY OF JAPAN

The history of Japan encompasses the history of the islands of Japan and the Japanese people, spanning the ancient history of the region to the modern history of Japan as a nation state. The first known written reference to Japan is in the brief information given in Twenty-Four Histories, a collection of Chinese historical texts, in the 1st century AD. However, there is evidence that suggests people were living on the islands of Japan since the upper Paleolithic period. Following the last ice-age, around 12,000 BC, the rich ecosystem of the Japanese Archipelago fostered human development. The earliest-known pottery belongs to the Jōmon period.

Contents:

1 Japanese prehistory
- o 1.1 Paleolithic Age

Aicient Japan
- o 2.1 Jōmon period
- o 2.2 Yayoi period
- o 2.3 Kofun period

3 Classical Japan
- o 3.1 Asuka period
- o 3.2 Nara period
- o 3.3 Heian period

4 Feudal Japan (1185-1868)

- 4.1 Kamakura period
- 4.2 Kemmu Restoration
- 4.3 Muromachi period
- 4.4 Sengoku period
- 4.5 Azuchi-Momoyama period

5 Edo period (1603-1868)
- 5.1 Seclusion
- 5.2 End of seclusion

6 Empire of Japan (1868-1945)
- 6.1 Meiji Restoration
- 6.2 Wars with China and Russia
- 6.3 Anglo-Japanese Alliance
- 6.4 World War I
- 6.5 Fascism in Japan
- 6.6 Second Sino-Japanese War and World War II

7 State of Japan (1945-present)
- 7.1 Occupation of Japan
- 7.2 After occupation during the Cold War
- 7.3 After the Cold War

8 Periodization

9 Regnal years
- 9.1 Other eras

10 See also

11 References

12 External links

Japanese prehistory:

Paleolithic Age:

Polished stone axes, excavated at Hinatabayashi B site, Shinano city, Nagano. Pre-Jōmon period, 30,000 BC. Tokyo National Museum

Main article: Japanese Paleolithic:

The Japanese Paleolithic age covers a lengthy period starting from around 100,000 to 30,000 B.C., when the earliest stone tool implements would have been found, and ending sometime around 12,000 B.C., at the end of the last ice age.

This timeline corresponds with the beginning of the Mesolithic Jōmon period. As the Jōmon period has a start date of around 35,000 B.C, it is most generally accepted.

The Japanese archipelago would become disconnected from the mainland continent after the last ice age, around 11,000 BC. After a hoax by an amateur researcher, Shinichi Fujimura, had been exposed, the Lower and Middle Paleolithic evidence reported by Fujimura and his associates has been rejected after thorough reinvestigation.

As a result of the fallout over the hoax, now only some Upper Paleolithic evidence (not associated with Fujimura) can possibly be considered as having been well established.

Ancient Japan.
Jōmon period. A Middle Jōmon vessel (3000–2000 BC)

Main article: Jōmon period:

The Jōmon period lasted from about 14,000 BC until 500 BC. The first signs of civilization and stable living patterns appeared around 14,000 BC with the Jōmon culture, characterized by a Mesolithic to Neolithic semi-sedentary hunter-gatherer lifestyle of wood stilt house and pit dwellings and a rudimentary form of agriculture.

Weaving was still unknown at the time and clothes were often made of furs. The Jōmon people started to make clay vessels, decorated with patterns made by impressing the wet clay with braided or un-braided cord and sticks. Based on radio-carbon dating, some of the oldest surviving examples of pottery in the world can be found in Japan along with daggers, jade, combs made of shells, and various other household items dated to the 11th millennium BC. Alternatively, the Metropolitan Museum of Art's Timeline of Art History notes "Carbon-14 testing of the earliest known shards has yielded a production date of about 10,500 BC, but because this date falls outside the known chronology of pottery development elsewhere in the world, such an early date is not generally accepted.

Calibrated radiocarbon measures of carbonized material from pottery artifacts: Fukui Cave 12500 +/- 350 BP and 12500 +/- 500 BP (Kamaki & Serizawa 1967), Kamikuroiwa rock shelter 12, 165 +/-350 years BP in Shikoku although the specific dating is disputed.

Clay figures known as dogū were also excavated. The household items

suggest trade routes existed with places as far away as Okinawa.[citation needed] DNA analysis suggests that the Ainu, an indigenous people that live in Hokkaidō and the northern part of Honshū, are descended from the Jōmon and thus represent descendants of the first inhabitants of Japan.
Yayoi period

Main article: Yayoi period;
A Yayoi period Dōtaku, 3rd century AD:

The Yayoi period lasted from about 400 or 300 BC to AD 250. This period followed the Jōmon period and completely supplanted it. This period is named after Yayoi town, the subsection of Bunkyō, Tokyo, where archaeological investigations uncovered its first recognized traces.

The start of the Yayoi period marked the influx of new practices such as weaving, rice farming, shamanism,[citation needed] and iron and bronze-making. Bronze and iron appear to have been introduced simultaneously into Yayoi Japan. Iron was mainly used for agricultural and other tools; whereas, ritual and ceremonial artifacts were mainly made of bronze. Some casting of bronze and iron began in Japan by about 100 BC, but the raw materials for both metals were introduced from the Asian continent.

Japan first appeared in written records in AD 57 with the following mention in China's Book of the Later Han: "Across the ocean from Lelang are the people of Wa. Formed from more than one hundred tribes, they come and pay tribute frequently". The book also recorded that Suishō, the king of Wa, presented slaves to the Emperor An of Han in 107. The Sanguo Zhi, written in the 3rd century, noted the country was the unification of some 30 small tribes or states and ruled by a shaman queen named Himiko of Yamataikoku.

During the Han and Wei dynasties, Chinese travelers to Kyūshū recorded its inhabitants and claimed that they were the descendants of the Grand Count (Tàibó) of the Wu. The inhabitants also show traits of the pre-sinicized Wu people with tattooing, teeth-pulling, and baby-carrying. The Sanguo Zhi records the physical descriptions which are similar to ones on haniwa statues, such as men with braided hair, tattooing, and women wearing large, single-piece clothing.

The Yoshinogari site in Kyūshū is the most famous archaeological site of the Yayoi period and reveals a large settlement continuously inhabited for several hundred years. Archaeological excavation has shown the most ancient parts to be from around 400 BC. It appears the inhabitants had frequent communication with the mainland and trade relations. Today, some reconstructed buildings stand in the park on the archaeological site of the Kofun period. Iron helmet & armour with gilt bronze decoration. It was the Kofun per, 5th century Tokyo National Museum.

Main article: Kofun period

The Kofun period (pronounced Kǒ Fǔn) began around 250 A.D., is named after the large tumulus burial mounds (kofun) that started appearing around that time.

The Kofun period (the "Kofun-Jidai") saw the establishment of strong military states, each of them was center around powerful clans (or zoku). The establishment of the dominant Yamato polity was centered in the provinces of Yamato and Kawachi from the 3rd Century A.D. till the 7th Century A.D., establishing the origin of the Japanese imperial lineage. And so the polity, by suppressing the clans and acquiring agricultural lands, maintained a strong influence in the western part of Japan.

Japan started to send tributes to Imperial China in the 5th century. In the Chinese history records, the polity was called Wa, and its five kings were recorded. Based upon the Chinese model, they developed a central administration and an imperial court system, with its society being organized into various occupation groups. Close relationships between the Three Kingdoms of Korea and Japan began during the middle of this period, around the end of the 4th century.

Classical Japan.

Asuka period:
Mural painting on the wall of the Takamatsuzuka Tomb, Asuka, Nara, 8th century

Main article: Asuka period:

During the Asuka period (538 to 710), the proto-Japanese Yamato polity gradually became a clearly centralized state, defining and applying a code of governing laws, such as the Taika Reforms and Taihō Code. The introduction of Buddhism led to the discontinuing of the practice of large kofun.

Buddhism was introduced to Japan in 538 by Baekje to which Japan provided military support, and was promoted by the ruling class. Prince

Shōtoku devoted his efforts to the spread of Buddhism and Chinese culture in Japan. He is credited with bringing relative peace to Japan through the proclamation of the Seventeen-article constitution, a Confucian style document that focused on the kinds of morals and virtues that were to be expected of government officials and the emperor's subjects. Buddhism would become a permanent part of Japanese culture.

A letter brought to the Emperor of China by an emissary from Japan in 607 stated that the "Emperor of the Land where the Sun rises (Japan) sends a letter to the Emperor of the land where Sun sets (China)" thereby implying an equal footing with China which angered the Chinese emperor. Nara period. The Great Buddha at Nara, 752 AD.

Main article: Nara period:

The Nara period of the 8th century marked the first emergence of a strong Japanese state. Following an imperial re-script by Empress Gemmei, the capital was moved to Heijō-kyō, present-day Nara, in 710. The city was modeled on Chang'an (now Xi'an), the capital of the Chinese Tang Dynasty.

During the Nara Period, political development was quite limited since members of the imperial family struggled for power with the Buddhist clergy as well as the regents, the Fujiwara clan. Japan did enjoy friendly relations with Silla as well as formal relationships with Tang China. In 784, the capital was moved again to Nagaoka-kyō to escape the Buddhist priests and then in 794 to Heian-kyō, present-day Kyōto.

Historical writing in Japan culminated in the early 8th century with the massive chronicles, the Kojiki (The Record of Ancient Matters, 712) and the Nihon Shoki (Chronicles of Japan, 720). These chronicles give a legendary account of Japan's beginnings, today known as the Japanese mythology. According to the myths contained in these chronicles, Japan was founded in 660 BC by the ancestral Emperor Jimmu, a direct descendant of the Shintō deity Amaterasu, or the Sun Goddess. The myths recorded that Jimmu started a line of emperors that remains to this day. Historians assume the myths partly describe historical facts, but the first emperor who actually existed was Emperor Ōjin, though the date of his reign is uncertain. Since the Nara period, actual political power has not been in the hands of the emperor but has instead been exercised at different times by the court nobility, warlords, the military and, more recently, the Prime Minister of Japan.

A handscroled painting dated circa 1130, illustrating a scene from the "Bamboo River" chapter of the Tale of Genji. Miniature model of Heian-kyō.

Main article: Heian period:

The Heian period, lasting from 794 to 1185, is the final period of classical Japanese history. It is considered the peak of the Japanese imperial court and noted for its art, especially its poetry and literature. In the early 11th century, Lady Murasaki wrote Japan's (and one of the world's) oldest surviving novels, The Tale of Genji. The Man'yōshū and Kokin Wakashū, the oldest existing collections of Japanese poetry, were compiled during this period.

Strong differences from mainland Asian cultures emerged (such as an indigenous writing system, the kana). Due to the decline of the Tang Dynasty, Chinese influence had reached its peak, and then effectively ended, with the last imperially sanctioned mission to Tang China in 838, although trade expeditions and Buddhist pilgrimages to China continued.

Political power in the imperial court was in the hands of powerful aristocratic families (kuge), especially the Fujiwara clan, who ruled under the titles Sesshō and Kampaku (imperial regents). The end of the period saw the rise of various military clans. The four most powerful clans were the Minamoto clan, the Taira clan, the Fujiwara clan, and the Tachibana clan. Towards the end of the 12th century, conflicts between these clans turned into civil war, such as the Hōgen and Heiji Rebellions, followed by the Genpei War, from which emerged a society led by samurai clans under the political rule of the shōgun.

Feudal Japan (1185-1868):

The "feudal" period of Japanese history, dominated by the powerful regional families (daimyō) and the military rule of warlords (shōgun), stretched from 1185 to 1868. The emperor remained but was mostly kept to a de jure figurehead ruling position, and the power of merchants was weak. This time is usually divided into periods following the reigning family of the shōgun.

Main article: Kamakura period:

The Kamakura period, 1185 to 1333, is a period that marks the governance of the Kamakura shogunate and the transition to the Japanese "medieval" era, a nearly 700-year period in which the emperor, the court, and the traditional central government were left intact but largely relegated to ceremonial functions. Civil, military, and judicial matters were controlled by the bushi (samurai) class, the most powerful of whom was the de facto national ruler, the shōgun. This period in Japan differed from the old shōen system in its pervasive military emphasis. Japanese samurai boarding Mongol ships in 1281

In 1185, Minamoto no Yoritomo defeated the rival Taira clan, and in 1192, Yoritomo was appointed Seii Tai-Shōgun by the emperor. Establishing a base of power in Kamakura, Yoritomo ruled as the first in a line of Kamakura shōgun. However, after Yoritomo's death, another warrior clan, the Hōjō, came to rule as shikken (regents) for the shōgun.

A traumatic event of the period was the Mongol invasions of Japan between 1274 and 1281, in which massive Mongol forces with superior naval technology and weaponry attempted a full-scale invasion of the Japanese islands. A famous typhoon referred to as kamikaze (translating as divine wind in Japanese) is credited with devastating both Mongol invasion forces in addition to the defensive measures the Japanese built on the island of Kyūshū. Although the Japanese were successful in stopping the Mongols, the invasion attempt had devastating domestic repercussions, leading to the extinction of the Kamakura shogunate. Kemmu Restoration.

Main articles: Kemmu Restoration and Nanboku-chō period:

In 1333, the Kamakura shogunate was overthrown in a coup d'état known as the Kemmu Restoration, led by Emperor Go-Daigo and his followers (Ashikaga Takauji, Nitta. Yoshisada, and Kusunoki Masashige). The Imperial House was restored to political influence, but this only lasted three years, ending when samurai opposed to Go-Daigo enthroned Emperor Kōgon. Muromachi period. Kinkaku-ji, Kyoto. 1397, in Kitayama period.

Main article: Muromachi period:

Kitayama period and Higashiyama period:

During the Muromachi period, the Ashikaga shogunate ruled for 237 years from 1336 to 1573. It was established by Ashikaga Takauji who seized political power from Emperor Go-Daigo, exiling him to Yoshino and ending the Kemmu restoration. The early years (1336 to 1392) of the Muromachi period are known as the Nanboku-chō (Northern and

Southern court) period because the imperial court was split in two. The Muromachi period ended in 1573 when the 15th and last shōgun, Ashikaga Yoshiaki, was driven out of the capital in Kyoto by Oda Nobunaga.

In the viewpoint of a cultural history, Kitayama period (14th end-15th first half clarification needed and Higashiyama period (15th second half-16th first half[clarification needed]) exist in Muromachi period. Sengoku period. Osaka Castle

Hasekura Tsunenaga and San Juan Bautista.

Sengoku period:

Nanban trade and Kirishitan:

The later years of the Muromachi period, 1467 to 1573, are also known as the Sengoku period (Period of Warring Kingdoms), a time of intense internal warfare, and corresponds with the period of the first contacts with the West—the arrival of Portuguese "Nanban" traders.

In 1543, a Portuguese ship, blown off its course to China, landed on Tanegashima Island. Firearms introduced by the Portuguese would bring the major innovation of the Sengoku period, culminating in the Battle of Nagashino where reportedly 3,000 arquebuses (the actual number is believed to be around 2,000) cut down charging ranks of samurai. During the following years, traders from Portugal, the Netherlands, England, and Spain arrived, as did Jesuit, Dominican, and Franciscan missionaries. Azuchi-Momoyama period.

Main article: Azuchi-Momoyama period:

The Azuchi-Momoyama period runs from approximately 1568 to 1603. The period, regarded as the late Warring Kingdoms period, marks the military reunification and stabilization of the country under a single political ruler, first by the campaigns of Oda Nobunaga who almost united Japan and achieved later by one of his generals, Toyotomi Hideyoshi. The name Azuchi-Momoyama comes from the names of their respective castles, Azuchi Castle and Momoyama Castle.

After having united Japan, Hideyoshi invaded Korea in an attempt to conquer Korea, China, and even India. However, after two unsuccessful campaigns towards the allied forces of Korea and China and his death, his forces retreated from the Korean Peninsula in 1598. Following his death, Japan experienced a short period of succession conflict. Tokugawa Ieyasu, one of the regents for Hideyoshi's young heir, emerged victorious at the Battle of Sekigahara and seized political power. Edo period (1603-1868).

Edo period:

Tokugawa Ieyasu, first shogun of the Tokugawa shogunate. "Bird's-eye view of Edo". (Hakushow Tachikawa1862).

During the Edo period, also called the Tokugawa period, the administration of the country was shared by over two hundred daimyō in a federation governed by the Tokugawa shogunate. The Tokugawa clan, leader of the victorious eastern army in the Battle of Sekigahara, was the most powerful of them and for fifteen generations monopolized the title of Sei-i Taishōgun (often shortened to shōgun). With their headquarters at Edo (present-day Tōkyō), the Tokugawa commanded the allegiance of the other daimyō, who in turn ruled their domains with a rather high degree of autonomy.

The Tokugawa shogunate carried out a number of significant policies. They placed the samurai class above the commoners: the agriculturists, artisans, and merchants. They enacted sumptuary laws limiting hair style, dress, and accessories. They organized commoners into groups of five and held all responsible for the acts of each individual. To prevent daimyō from rebelling, the shōguns required them to maintain lavish residences in Edo and live at these residences on a rotating schedule; carry out expensive processions to and from their domains; contribute to the upkeep of shrines, temples, and roads; and seek permission before repairing their castles.

This 265-year span directly prior to seclusion was called "A peaceful state". Cultural achievement was high during this period, and many artistic developments took place. Most significant among them were the ukiyo-e form of wood-block print and the kabuki and bunraku theaters. Also, many of the most famous works for the koto and shakuhachi date from this time period. Seclusion. The following text needs to be harmonized with text in Sakoku.

Main article: Sakoku:

It was Japan's first treatise on Western anatomy, published in 1774, an example of Rangaku. During the early part of the 17th century, the shogunate suspected that foreign traders and missionaries were actually forerunners of a military conquest by European powers. Christianity had spread in Japan, especially among peasants, and the shogunate suspected the loyalty of Christian peasants towards their daimyō, severely persecuting them. This led to a revolt by persecuted peasants and Christians in 1637 known as the Shimabara Rebellion which saw 30,000 Christians, rōnin, and peasants facing a massive samurai army of more than 100,000 sent from Edo. The rebellion was crushed at a high cost to the shōgun's army.

After the eradication of the rebels at Shimabara, the shogunate placed foreigners under progressively tighter restrictions. It monopolized foreign policy and expelled traders, missionaries, and foreigners with the exception of the Dutch and Chinese merchants who were restricted to the man-made island of Dejima in Nagasaki Bay and several small trading outposts outside the country. However, during this period of isolation (Sakoku) that began in 1635, Japan was much less cut off from the rest of the world than is commonly assumed, and some acquisition of western knowledge occurred under the Rangaku system. Russian encroachments from the north led the shogunate to extend direct rule to Hokkaidō, Sakhalin and the Kuriles in 1807, but the policy of exclusion continued.

End of seclusion:

It was landing of Commodore Perry, officers & men of the squadron, to meet the Imperial commissioners at Yokohama July 14, 1853. Lithograph by Sarony & Co., 1855, after W. Heine.

Main article: Bakumatsu:

The policy of isolation lasted for more than 200 years. In 1844, William II of the Netherlands sent a message urging Japan to open its doors which was rejected by the Japanese. On July 8, 1853, Commodore Matthew Perry of the United States Navy with four warships—the Mississippi, Plymouth, Saratoga, and Susquehanna—steamed into the bay in Yokohama and displayed the threatening power of his ships' cannons during a Christian burial which the Japanese observed. He requested that Japan open to trade with the West. These ships became known as the kurofune, the Black Ships.

The following year at the Convention of Kanagawa on March 31, 1854, Perry returned with seven ships and demanded that the shōgun sign the Treaty of Peace and Amity, establishing formal diplomatic relations between Japan and the United States. Within five years, Japan had signed similar treaties with other Western countries. The Harris Treaty was signed with the United States on July 29, 1858. These treaties were unequal, having been forced on Japan through gunboat diplomacy, and were interpreted by the Japanese as a sign of Western imperialism taking hold of the rest of the Asian continent. Among other measures, they gave the Western nations unequivocal control of tariffs on imports and the right of extraterritoriality to all of their visiting nationals. They would remain a sticking point in Japan's relations with the West up to the turn of the century.

Empire of Japan (1868-1945).

Empire of Japan:
Beginning in 1868, Japan undertook political, economic, and cultural reforms, emerging as a unified and centralized state known as the Empire of Japan (also Imperial Japan or Prewar Japan). This 77-year period, which lasted until 1945, was a time of imperialism and absolutism. Japan became an imperial power, colonizing Korea and Taiwan. Meiji Restoration.

Main articles: Meiji Restoration and Meiji period:
It was Samurai of the Satsuma clan, during the Boshin War period. Coloured photograph by Felice Beato "the seed is sown, and Japan will move, upon the whole, in the direction of progress".

Andrew Carnegie, Round the World (1878):
Renewed contact with the West precipitated a profound alteration of Japanese society. Importantly, within the context of Japan's subsequent aggressive militarism, the signing of the treaties was viewed as profoundly humiliating and a source of national shame. The Tokugawa shōgun was forced to resign, and soon after the Boshin War of 1868, the emperor was restored to power, beginning a period of fierce nationalism and intense socio-economic restructuring known as the Meiji Restoration. The Tokugawa system was abolished, the military was modernized, and numerous Western institutions were adopted–including a Western legal system and quasi-parliamentary constitutional government as outlined in the Meiji Constitution. This constitution was modeled on the constitution of the German Empire. While many aspects of the Meiji Restoration were adopted directly from Western institutions, others, such as the dissolution of the feudal system and removal of the shogunate, were processes that had begun long before the arrival of Perry. Nonetheless, Perry's intervention is widely viewed as a pivotal moment in Japanese history.

Russian pressure from the north appeared again after Muraviev had gained Outer Manchuria at Aigun (1858) and Peking (1860). This led to heavy Russian pressure on Sakhalin which the Japanese eventually yielded in exchange for the Kuril islands (1875). The Ryukyu Islands were similarly secured in 1879, establishing the borders within which Japan would "enter the World". In 1898, the last of the unequal treaties with Western powers was removed, signalling Japan's new status among the nations of the world. In a few decades by reforming and modernizing social, educational, economic, military, political and industrial systems, the Emperor Meiji's "controlled revolution" had transformed a feudal and isolated state into a world power. Significantly, the impetus for this change was the belief that Japan had to compete with the West both industrially and militarily to achieve equality. Wars with China and Russia.

Main article: Foreign relations of Meiji Japan:
Japanese intellectuals of the late-Meiji period espoused the concept of a "line of advantage", an idea that would help to justify Japanese foreign policy at the turn of the century. According to this principle, embodied in the slogan fukoku kyōhei, Japan would be vulnerable to aggressive Western imperialism unless it extended a line of advantage beyond its borders which would help to repel foreign incursions and strengthen the Japanese economy. Emphasis was especially placed on Japan's "pre-eminent interests" in the Korean Peninsula, once famously described as a "dagger pointed at the heart of Japan". It was tensions over Korea and Manchuria, respectively that led Japan to become involved in the first Sino-Japanese War with China in 1894–1895 and the Russo-Japanese War with Russia in 1904–1905.

The war with China made Japan the world's first Eastern, modern imperial power, and the war with Russia proved that a Western power could be defeated by an Eastern state. The aftermath of these two wars left Japan the dominant power in the Far East with a sphere of influence extending over southern Manchuria and Korea, which was formally annexed as part of the Japanese Empire in 1910. Japan had also gained half of Sakhalin Island from Russia. The results of these wars established Japan's dominant interest in Korea, while giving it the Pescadores Islands, Formosa (now Taiwan), and the Liaodong Peninsula in Manchuria, which was eventually retrocede in the "humiliating" Triple Intervention.

Over the next decade, Japan would flaunt its growing prowess, including a very significant contribution to the Eight-Nation Alliance formed to quell China's Boxer Rebellion. Many Japanese, however, believed their new empire was still regarded as inferior by the Western powers, and they sought a means of cementing their international standing. This set the climate for growing tensions with Russia, which would continually intrude into Japan's "line of advantage" during this time.

Anglo-Japanese Alliance:

The Anglo-Japanese Alliance treaty was signed between the United Kingdom and Japan on January 30, 1902, and announced on February 12, 1902. It was renewed in 1905 and 1911 before its demise in 1921 and its termination in 1923. It was a military alliance between the two countries that threatened Russia and Germany. Due to this alliance, Japan entered World War I on the side of Great Britain. Japan attacked German bases in China and sent troops to the Mediterranean in 1917. Through this treaty, there was also great cultural exchange between the two countries. World War I.

Early Modern Japan, Marunouchi, Tokyo 1920:

In a manner perhaps reminiscent of its participation in quelling the Boxer Rebellion at the turn of the century, Japan entered World War I and declared war on the Central Powers. Though Japan's role in World War I was limited largely to attacking German colonial outposts in East Asia, it took advantage of the opportunity to expand its influence in Asia and its territorial holdings in the Pacific. Acting virtually independently of the civil government, the Japanese navy seized Germany's Micronesian colonies. It also attacked and occupied the German coaling port of Qingdao in the Chinese Shandong peninsula.

Japan went to the peace conference at Versailles in 1919 as one of the great military and industrial powers of the world and received official recognition as one of the "Big Five" of the new international order. It joined the League of Nations and received a mandate over Pacific islands north of the Equator formerly held by Germany. Japan was also involved in the post-war Allied intervention in Russia, occupying Russian (Outer) Manchuria and also north Sakhalin (with its rich oil reserves). It was the last Allied power to withdraw from the interventions against Soviet Russia (doing so in 1925).

The post–World War I era brought Japan unprecedented prosperity. Fascism in Japan.

Main article: Statism in Shōwa Japan:

During the 1910s and 1920s, Japan progressed towards democracy movements known as 'Taishō Democracy'. However, parliamentary government was not rooted deeply enough to withstand the economic and political pressures of the late 1920s and 1930s during the Depression period, and its state became increasingly militarized. This was due to the increasing powers of military leaders and was similar to the actions some European nations were taking leading up to World War II. These shifts in power were made possible by the ambiguity and imprecision of the Meiji Constitution, particularly its measure that the legislative body was answerable to the Emperor and not the people. The Kodoha, a militarist faction, even attempted a coup d'état known as the February 26 Incident, which was crushed after three days by Emperor Shōwa.

Party politics came under increasing fire because it was believed they were divisive to the nation and promoted self-interest where unity was needed. As a result, the major parties voted to dissolve themselves and were absorbed into a single party, the Imperial Rule Assistance Association (IRAA), which also absorbed many prefectural organizations such as women's clubs and neighbourhood associations. However, this umbrella organization did not have a cohesive political agenda and factional in-fighting persisted throughout its existence, meaning Japan did not devolve into a totalitarian state. The IRAA has been likened to a sponge, in that it could soak everything up, but there is little one could do with it afterwards. Its creation was precipitated by a series of domestic crises, including the advent of the Great Depression in the 1930s and the actions of extremists such as the members of the Cherry Blossom Society, who enacted the May 15 Incident.

Second Sino-Japanese War and World War II:

Main articles: Germany–Japan relations, Second Sino-Japanese war, Pacific War, Greater East Asia Co-Prosperity Sphere, and Home front during World War II⊠#Japan

The Imperial Japanese Navy's Yamato, the heaviest battleship in history, 1941.

Under the pretext of the Manchurian Incident, Lieutenant Colonel Kanji Ishiwara invaded Inner (Chinese) Manchuria in 1931, an action the Japanese government ratified with the creation of the puppet state of Manchukuo under the last Chinese emperor, Pu Yi. As a result of international condemnation of the incident, Japan resigned from the League of Nations in 1933. After several more similar incidents fuel by an expansionist military, the second Sino-Japanese War began in 1937 after the Marco Polo Bridge Incident.

During the pre-1945 Shōwa period, according to the Meiji Constitution, the Emperor had the "supreme command of the Army and the Navy" (Article 11). From 1937, Emperor Shōwa became supreme commander of the Imperial General Headquarters, by which the military decisions were made. This ad-hoc body consisted of the chief and vice chief of the Army, the minister of the Army, the chief and vice chief of the Navy, the minister of the Navy, the inspector general of military aviation, and the inspector general of military training.

Having joined the Anti-Comintern Pact in 1936, Japan formed the Axis Pact with Germany and Italy on September 27, 1940. Many Japanese politicians believed war with the Occident to be inevitable due to inherent cultural differences and Western imperialism. Japanese imperialism was then justified by the revival of the traditional concept of hakko ichiu, the divine right of the emperor to unite and rule the world.

Japan fought the Soviet Union in 1938 in the Battle of Lake Khasan and in 1939 in the Battle of Khalkhin Gol. Comprehensive defeat of the Japanese by the Soviets led by Zhukov in the latter battle led to the signing of the Soviet–Japanese Neutrality Pact.

Tensions were mounting with the U.S. as a result of public outcry over Japanese aggression and reports of atrocities in China, such as the infamous Nanjing Massacre. In retaliation to the invasion of French Indochina the U.S. began an embargo on such goods as petroleum products and scrap iron. On July 25, 1941, all Japanese assets in the US were frozen. Because Japan's military might, especially the Navy, was dependent on their dwindling oil reserves, this action had the contrary effect of increasing Japan's dependence on and hunger for new acquisitions.

Many civil leaders of Japan, including Prime Minister Konoe Fumimaro, believed a war with America would end in defeat, but felt the concessions demanded by the U.S. would almost certainly relegate Japan from the ranks of the World Powers, leaving it prey to Western collusion. Civil leaders offered political compromises in the form of the Amau Doctrine, dubbed the "Japanese Monroe Doctrine" that would have given the Japanese free rein with regards to war with China. These offers were flatly rejected by U.S. Secretary of State Cordell Hull; the military leaders instead vied for quick military action.

Most military leaders such as Osami Nagano, Kotohito Kan'in, Hajime Sugiyama and Hideki Tōjō believed that war with the Occident was inevitable. They finally convinced Emperor Shōwa to sanction on November 1941 an attack plan against U.S., Great Britain and the Netherlands. However, there were dissenters in the ranks about the wisdom of that option, most notably Admiral Yamamoto Isoroku and Prince Takamatsu. They pointedly warned that at the beginning of hostilities with the US, the Empire would have the advantage for six months, after which Japan's defeat in a prolonged war would be almost certain. There were planes from the Japanese aircraft carrier Shokaku that prepared the attack on Pearl Harbor.

The Americans were expecting an attack in the Philippines (and stationed troops appropriate to this conjecture), but on Yamamoto Isoroku's advice, Japan made the decision to attack Pearl Harbor where it would make the most damage in the least amount of time. The United States believed that Japan would never be so bold as to attack so close to its home base (Hawaii had not yet become a state) and was taken completely by surprise.

The attack on Pearl Harbor, sanctioned by Emperor Shōwa on December 1, 1941, occurred on December 7 (December 8 in Japan) and the Japanese were successful in their surprise attack. Although the Japanese won the battle, the attack proved a long-term strategic disaster that actually did relatively little lasting damage to the U.S. military and provoked the United States to retaliate with full commitment against Japan and its allies. At the same time as the Pearl Harbor attack, the Japanese army attacked colonial Hong Kong and occupied it for nearly four years.

While Nazi Germany was in the middle of its Blitzkrieg through Europe, Japan was following suit in Asia. In addition to already having colonised Taiwan and Manchuria, the Japanese Army invaded and captured most of the coastal Chinese cities such as Shanghai, and had conquered French Indochina (Vietnam, Laos, Cambodia, British Malaya (Brunei, Malaysia, Singapore) as well as the Dutch East Indies (Indonesia) while Thailand entered into a loose alliance with Japan. They had also conquered Burma and reached the borders of India and Australia, conducting air raids on the port of Darwin, Australia. Japan had soon established an empire stretching over much of the Pacific.

Atomic cloud over Hiroshima, 1945.

However as Admiral Yamamoto warned, Japan's six month window of military advantage after Pearl Harbor ended with the Japanese Navy's offensive ability being crippled at the hands of the American Navy in the Battle of Midway, which turned the tide against them. After almost four years of war resulting in the loss of three million Japanese lives, the atomic bombings of Hiroshima and Nagasaki, the daily air raids on Tokyo, Osaka, Nagoya, Yokohama, the destruction of all other major cities (except Kyoto, Nara, and Kamakura, for their historical importance), and finally the Soviet Union's declaration of war on Japan the day before the second atomic bomb was dropped, Japan signed an instrument of surrender on the USS Missouri in Tokyo Harbour on September 2, 1945. Symbolically, the deck of the Missouri was furnished bare except for two American flags. One had flown on the mast of Commodore Perry's ship when he had sailed into that same bay nearly a century earlier to urge the opening of Japan's ports to foreign trade. The other U.S. flag came off the battleship while anchored in Tokyo Bay, it had not flown over the White House or the Capitol Building on 7 December 1941, it was "just a plain ordinary GI flag." State of Japan (1945-present).

Main article: Postwar Japan:

By collapse of the Empire of Japan, Japan was changed to a democratic state, the State of Japan, more commonly the Postwar Japan (post–World War II Japan). During the postwar period, Japan became an economic power state. But, this period is characterized by the US-Japan Alliance such as the United States Forces Japan. It was the occupation of Japan. General MacArthur and Emperor Hirohito.

Main article: Occupation of Japan:

As a result of its defeat of World War II, the Empire of Japan was dissolved. Japan lost all of its overseas possessions and retained only the home islands. Manchukuo was dissolved, and Inner Manchuria and Taiwan were returned to the Republic of China; Korea was taken under the control of the UN; southern Sakhalin and the Kuriles were occupied by the U.S.S.R.; and the United States became the sole administering authority of the Ryukyu, Bonin, and Volcano Islands. The International Military Tribunal for the Far East (Tokyo Trial), an international war crimes tribunal, was held, in which seven politicians were executed. Emperor Hirohito was not convicted, but instead was enthroned as the emperor of the new state.

The 1972 reversion of Okinawa completed the United States' return of control of these islands to Japan. Japan continues to protest for the corresponding return of the Kuril Islands from Russia.

Defeat came for a number of reasons. The most important is probably Japan's underestimation of the industrious-military capabilities of the U.S. The U.S. recovered from its initial setback at Pearl Harbor much quicker than the Japanese expected, and their sudden counterattack came as a blow to Japanese morale. U.S. output of military products was also much higher than Japanese counterparts over the course of the war. Another reason was factional in-fighting between the Army and Navy, which led to poor intelligence and cooperation. This was compounded as the Japanese forces found they had overextended themselves, leaving Japan itself vulnerable to attack. Another important factor is Japan's underestimation of resistance in China, which Japan whose claims would be conquered in three months. The prolonged war was both militarily and economically disastrous for Japan.

After the war, Japan was placed under international control of the American-led Allied powers in the Asia-Pacific region through General Douglas MacArthur as Supreme Commander of the Allied Powers. This was the first time since the unification of Japan that the island nation was successfully occupied by a foreign power. Some high officers of the Shōwa regime were prosecuted and convicted by the International Military Tribunal for the Far East. However, Emperor Shōwa, all members of the imperial family implicated in the war such as prince Asaka, prince Chichibu, prince Takeda, prince Higashikuni, prince Fushimi, as well as Shirō Ishii and all members of unit 731 were exonerated from criminal prosecutions by MacArthur.

Entering the Cold War with the Korean War, Japan came to be seen as an important ally of the US government. Political, economic, and social reforms were introduced, such as an elected Japanese Diet (legislature) and expanded suffrage. The country's constitution took effect on May 3, 1947. The United States and 45 other Allied nations signed the Treaty of Peace with Japan in September 1951. The U.S. Senate ratified the treaty on March 20, 1952, and under the terms of the treaty, Japan regained full sovereignty on April 28, 1952.

Under the terms of the peace treaty and later agreements, the United States maintains naval bases at Sasebo, Okinawa and at Yokosuka. A portion of the U.S. Pacific Fleet, including one aircraft carrier (currently USS George Washington (CVN-73)), is based at Yokosuka. This arrangement is partially intended to provide for the defense of Japan, as the treaty and the new Japanese constitution imposed during the occupation severely restrict the size and purposes of Japanese Self-Defense Forces in the modern period.

After occupation during the Cold War
Main article: Post-Occupation of Japan:

After a series of realignment of political parties, the conservative Liberal Democratic Party (LDP) and the leftist Social Democratic Party (SDP) were formed in 1955. The political map in Japan had been largely unaltered until early 1990s and LDP had been the largest political party in the national politics. LDP politicians and government bureaucrats focused on economic policy. From the 1950s to the 1980s, Japan experienced its rapid development into a major economic power, through a process often referred to as the Japanese post-war economic miracle.

Japan's biggest postwar political crisis took place in 1960 over the revision of the Japan-United States Mutual Security Assistance Pact. As the new Treaty of Mutual Cooperation and Security was concluded, which renewed the United States role as military protector of Japan, massive street protests and political upheaval occurred, and the cabinet resigned a month after the Diet's ratification of the treaty. Thereafter, political turmoil subsided. Japanese views of the United States, after years of mass protests over nuclear armaments and the mutual defense pact, improved by 1972 with the reversion of United States-occupied Okinawa to Japanese sovereignty and the winding down of the Vietnam War.

Japan had re-established relations with the Republic of China after World War II, and cordial relations were maintained with the nationalist government when it was relocated to Taiwan, a policy that won Japan the enmity of the People's Republic of China, which was established in 1949. After the general warming of relations between China and Western countries, especially the United States, which shocked Japan with its sudden rapprochement with Beijing in 1971, Tokyo established relations with Beijing in 1972. Close cooperation in the economic sphere followed. Japan's relations with the Soviet Union continued to be problematic after the war, but a Joint Declaration between Japan and the USSR ending the state of war and re-establishing diplomatic relations was signed October 19, 1956.[19] The main object of dispute was the Soviet occupation of what Japan calls its Northern Territories, the two most southerly islands in the Kurils (Etorofu and Kunashiri) and Shikotan and the Habomai Islands, which were seized by the Soviet Union in the closing days of World War II.

Throughout the postwar period, Japan's economy continued to boom, with results far outstripping expectations. Given a massive boost by the Korean War, in which it acted as a major supplier to the UN force, Japan's economy embarked on a prolonged period of extremely rapid growth, led by the manufacturing sectors. Japan emerged as a significant power in many economic spheres, including steel working, car manufacturing and the manufacturing of electronic goods. Japan rapidly caught up with the West in foreign trade, GNP, and general quality of life. These achievements were underscored by the 1964 Tokyo Olympic Games and the Osaka International Exposition in 1970. The high economic growth and political tranquility of the mid to late 1960s were tempered by the quadrupling of oil prices by the OPEC in 1973. Almost completely dependent on imports for petroleum, Japan experienced its first recession since World War II. Another serious problem was Japan's growing trade surplus, which reached record heights during Nakasone's first term. The United States pressured Japan to remedy the imbalance, demanding that Tokyo raise the value of the yen and open its markets further to facilitate more imports from the United States after the Cold War.

Main article: Heisei period:

Japan after the Cold War is also called as the Heisei period, which starts from the year of the Revolutions of Eastern Europe. 1989 marked one of the most rapid economic growth spurts in Japanese history. With a strong yen and a favourable exchange rate with the dollar, the Bank of Japan kept interest rates low, sparking an investment boom that drove Tokyo property values up sixty percent within the year. Shortly before New Year's Day, the Nikkei 225 reached its record high of 39,000. By 1991, it had fallen to 15,000, signifying the end of Japan's famed bubble economy. Unemployment ran reasonably high, but not at crisis levels. Rather than suffer large scale unemployment and lay-offs, Japan's labour market suffered in more subtle, yet no less profound effects that were nonetheless difficult to gauge statistically. During the prosperous times, jobs were seen as long term even to the point of being life long. In contrast, Japan during the lost decade saw a marked increase in temporary and part time work which only promised employment for short periods and marginal benefits. This also created a generational gap, as those who had entered the labour market prior to the lost decade usually retained their employment and benefits, and were effectively insulated from the economic slowdown, whereas younger workers who entered the market a few years later suffered the brunt of its effects.

In a series of financial scandals of the LDP, a coalition led by Morihiro Hosokawa took power in 1993. Hosokawa succeed legislating new plurality voting election law instead of the stalemated multi-member constituency election system. However, the coalition collapsed the next year as parties had gathered to simply overthrow LDP and lacked a unified position on almost every social issue. The LDP returned to the government in 1996, when it helped to elect Social Democrat Tomiichi Murayama as prime minister.

The Great Hanshin earthquake hit Kobe on January 17, 1995. 6,000 people were killed and 44,000 were injured. 250,000 houses were destroyed or burned in a fire. The amount of damage total more than ten trillion yen. In March of the same year the doomsday cult Aum Shinrikyo attacked on the Tokyo subway system with saran gas and killed 12 and hundreds were injured. Later the investigation revealed that the cult was responsible for dozens of murders that occurred prior to the gas attacks.

Junichiro Koizumi was president of the LDP and Prime Minister of Japan from April 2001 to September 2006. Koizumi enjoyed high approval ratings. He was known as an economic reformer and he privatized the national postal system. Koizumi also had an active involvement in the War on Terrorism, sending 1,000 soldiers of the Japan Self-Defense Forces to help in Iraq's reconstruction after the Iraq War, the biggest overseas troop deployment since World War II.

The ruling coalition is formed by the liberal Democratic Party of Japan (DPJ), the leftist Social Democratic Party and the conservative People's New Party. The opposition is formed by the liberal conservative Liberal Democratic Party (LDP). Other parties are the New Komeito Party, a theocratic citation was needed. Buddhist political party based on the Buddhist sect Sōka Gakkai and the Japanese Communist Party. On 2 June 2010 Prime Minister Yukio Hatoyama officially resigned from his position as leader of the DPJ, citing the failure to fulfill his campaign promise of removing a U.S. base from the island of Okinawa as his main reason for stepping down.

The government of Japan didn't want any more war and that was because the United States had dropped two Atom Bombs on them and only then they would surrender. Now it was a new area for them to do good things for their people and the rest of the world would be at their side. They knew that hard work would bring their nation up to standard.

On March 11, 2011, Japan suffered the strongest earthquake in its recorded history, affecting the north-east area of Honshu. The magnitude 9.0 quake was aggravated by a tsunami and also caused numerous fires and damaged several nuclear reactors. On March 12, 2011 reactor 1 at the Fukushima Nuclear Plant suffered a build-up of hydrogen gas, and caused an explosion. On March 13, 2011 there was another explosion, at reactor 3. Radiation levels in the air were below legal limits, however. On March 15, 2011, the Fukushima plant experienced another explosion, this time at reactor 2. There was also a fire at reactor 4. There was a brief spike of radiation, but this then fell back below legal limits. It has since been announced that temperatures in reactors 5 and 6 are rising.

CHAPTER ONE

It was if the island of Japan was cursed, and the residents of Japan knew what was going to happen again, and it would hit them hard this time. The force of this dreadful demon had hit them hard again, taking away many of their friend and family. Their dreams and their lives would be taken away again, and they didn't think they deserved that sort of bad treatment. But they lived on a dangerous island of Japan, or may be they were cursed by the Gods.

The Great Hanshin earthquake of Kobe was their first encounter, and they had to deal with it. They had a system which told the people they were in danger because an earthquake was on its way. They knew what to do, because they had so much practice before with earthquakes in the past. They had the practice of fighting the earthquake and burying their dead, and life would go on the same way as before. That would be their history of time, and no one would be able to stop it, as it would be in the hands of time.

The earthquake occurred on Tuesday January 17, 1995 at 0546 JST (16 January at 20.46 UTC). It happened in the southern part of Hyogo Prefecture, Japan. It measured 6.8 on the moment magnitude scale (USGS), and Mj 7.3 (adjusted from 7.2 on JMA magnitude. They knew the earthquake was coming and they were prepared for it, but the earthquake was not prepared for them. It had to do its job and shake their world in pieces.

The people of Japan had a system, and they knew exactly what to do and how they would face the earthquake. They knew it would be a life and a death situation. They waited and they prayed that when the earthquake passed they would still have their precious lives. They really knew what the outcome would be before it happened.

The tremors lasted for about 20 seconds and those seconds seemed a long time to them, and damage to property and some persons would be killed or injured. Their lives would be in their hands of the Gods.

The focus of the earthquake was located 15 km beneath its epicenter, on the northern end of Awaji Island, 20 km away from the city of Kobe.

In the second score, approximately 6,434 people lost their lives (final estimate as of December 22, 2005 and about 4,600 of the people lost their lives from Kobe. It seemed at the time that the earthquake had a revenge on Kobe, a city among many cities, Kobe with its population of 1.5 million people. The people of Kobe were used to earthquakes, but this second time they were hit again and the quake took a lot of the people away, and it did major damages to their property. They felt they were cursed, but they were aware that they could be hit again by another earthquake.

It was the closest to the epicenter and it was hit by the strongest tremors. At that time that was Japan's worst earthquake since the Great Kanto earthquake in 1923, which claimed 140,000 lives. It caused approximately ten trillion yen in damage, 2.5% of Japan's GDP at that time. Based on the average currency conversion rate over the following 500 days of 97,545 yen per USD, the quake caused $102.5 billion in damage.

Damage from the Great Hanshin Earthquake is kept intact at the Earthquake Memorial Park near the port of Kobe. The elevated Hanshin Expressway, in the background, was partially toppled by the earthquake.

It was the first time that earthquake tremors in Japan were officially measured as seismic intensity (shindo in Japanese) of the highest Level 7 on the scale of Japan Meteorological Agency (JMA.

Note: After this earthquake, seismic intensity observation in Japan was fully mechanized (from April 1996) and JMA seismic intensity Levels 5 and 6 were each divided into 2 levels (from October 1996).

An on-the spot investigation by JMA concluded that tremors by this earthquake were seismic intensity of Level 7 in particular areas in northern Awaji Island (now Awaji City) and in the cities of Kobe, Ashiya, Nishinomiya and Takarazuka.

Tremors were valued at seismic intensity of Levels 6 to 4 at observation points in Kansai, Chugoku, Shikoku and Chubu regions.

At level 6 in cities of Sumoto (in Awaji) and Kone (both in Hyogo Prefecture).

At level 5 in the cities of Yoyooka (in Hyogo Prefecture), Hikone (in Shiga Prefecture) and Kyoto.

At level 4 in the prefectures of Hyogo, Shiga, Kyoto, Fukui, Gifu, Mie, Osaka, Nara, Wakayama, Tottori, Okayama, Hiroshima, Tokushima, Kagawa and Kochi.

Foreshocks and aftershocks:

The Mj 7.3 earthquake struck at 05.46 JST on the morning of 17 January 1995. It lasted for 20 seconds. During this time the south side of the Nojima Fault moved 1.5m to the right and 1.2 meters downwards. This was because the earthquake's focus was near the surface and its epicenter so near Kobe.

There were four foreshocks, beginning with the largest (Mj 3.7) at 18.28 on the previous day.

Within five weeks, about 50 aftershocks (Mj 4.0 or greater) were observed.

By May 23, 1995: 1983 aftershocks in total, 249 felt.

By October 31, 1995: 2309 aftershocks in total, 302 felt.

By October 31, 1996: 2522 aftershocks in total, 408 felt.

Damage:

The effects can be divided into primary and secondary effects. Primary effects include the collapse of the 200,000 buildings, the collapse of 1 km of the Hanshin Expressway, and destination of 120 of the 150 quays in the port of Kobe. Secondary effects included disruption of the electricity supply. Residents were afraid to return home because of aftershocks that lasted several days (74 of which were strong enough to be felt).

Damage in cities and suburbs:

The majority of deaths, over 4,000, occurred in cities and the suburbs in Hyogo Prefecture. One of the five of the buildings in the worst-hit area were completely destroyed (or rendered uninhabitable). About 22% of the offices in the central business district were rendered unusable and over half of the houses in that area were deemed unfit to live in. High rise buildings that were built after the modern 1981 building code suffered a little however, those that were not constructed to those standards suffered serious structural damage. Most of the older traditional houses had heavy tiled roofs which weighed around 2 tons, intended to resist the frequent typhoons that plagued Kobe, but they were only held up by a light wood support frame. When the wood supports gave way, the roof crushed the un-reinforced walls and the floors in a "pancake" collapse. Newer homes have reinforced walls and lighter roofs to avoid this, but are more susceptible to typhoons.

The extent of the damage was much greater than the Northridge earthquake in Los Angles, which, by coincidence, had occurred exactly one year before. The different was in part due to the type of ground beneath Kobe and the construction of its buildings (e.g. many un-reinforced masonry buildings collapsed). Also, at about 7.2 the intensity of the quake was greater than the approximately 6.6 of Northridge. The immediate population bases of the two areas (Kobe area and San Fernando Valley of Los Angles) were roughly the same – about 2 million, however only 72 people died in the Northridge quake compared to the more than 6,000 in Kobe.

It is noted that some of the older houses weren't build for that sort of weather, and the houses collapsed at the slightest turn of a typhoon, and when that happened, the people in that area would have a great struggle to survive, but with all their strength they held on to survival.

Transportation infrastructure damage:
The damage to highways and subways was the most graphic image of the earthquake, and images of the collapsed elevated Hanshin Expressway made front pages of newspapers worldwide. Most people in Japan believed those structures to be relatively safe from earthquake damage by design. Through the initial belief that construction had been negligent, and it was later shown that most of the collapsed structures were constructed properly to the building codes in force in the 1960s. However, the 1960s regulations had already been discovered to be inadequate and revised several times, and the latest revision was in 1981, which proved to be effective but it was only applied to new structures.

Ten spans of the Hanshin Expressway Route 43 in three locations in Kobe Nishinomiya were knocked over by a blowing a link that carried forty percent of Osaka-Kobe road traffic. Half of the elevated express's piers were damage in some way, and the entire route was not reopened until September 30, 1996. Three bridges on the less heavily used Route 2 were damaged, but the highway was reopened well ahead of Route 43 and served as one of the main intercity road links for a time. The Meishin Expressway was only lightly damaged, but was closed during the day until February 17, 1995, so that emergency vehicles could easily access the hardest-hit areas to the west. It wasn't until July 29 that all four lanes were open to traffic along one section (Kitamura, Yamamoto and Fujii 1998:240). Many surface highways were clogged for some time due to the collapse of higher-capacity elevated highways.

Most railways in the region were also damaged. It was in the aftermath of the earthquake, that only 30% of the Osaka-Kobe railways tracks were operational. Daikai Station on the Kobe Rapid Railway line collapsed, bringing down part of National Route 30 above it. Wooden supports collapsed inside supposedly solid concrete pilings under the track of the Shinkansen high-speed rail line, causing the entire line to shut down. However, the railways rebounded quickly after the quake, reaching 80% operability in one month.

Artificial islands in Kobe suffered some subsidence due to liquefaction of soil, and water breaking to the surface did not come from the sea. However, the newly-completed artificial island supporting Kansai International Airport was not significantly affected, due to being further away from the epicenter and because it was built to the latest standards. The Akashi Kaikyo Bridge, under construction near the earthquake's epicenter, was not damaged but was reportedly lengthened by a full meter due to horizontal displacement along the activated tectonic fault.

Response:

In the aftermath, both citizens and specialists lost faith in the technology of their early warning systems and earthquake construction techniques. The national government of Japan was criticized for not acting quickly enough to save many people, for poorly managing Japanese volunteers, and initially refusing help from foreign nations, including the United States, South Korea, Mongolia, and the United Kingdom. The language barriers and the obvious lack of Japanese medical licensing by foreign volunteers were cited as justification. In response to the widespread devastation, the Japanese government increased it spending on earthquake-resistant building structures.

Local response:

Local hospitals struggled to keep up with the demand for medical treatment, largely due to collapsed or obstructed "lifelines" (roads) that kept supplies and personnel from reaching the affected areas. People were forced to wait in corridors due to the overcrowding and lack of space. Some people had to be operated on in waiting rooms and corridors.

Approximately 1.2 million volunteers were involved in relief efforts during the first three months following the earthquake. Retailers such as Daiei and 7-Eleven used their existing supply networks to provide necessities in affected areas, while NTT and Motorola provided free telephone service for victims. Even the Yamaguchi-gumi yakaza syndicate was involved in distributing food and supplies to needy victims.

To help speed the recovery effort, the government closed most of the Hanshin Expressway network to private vehicles from 6:00 a.m. to 8:00 p.m. daily and limited traffic to buses, taxis and other designated vehicles (Kitamura, Yamamoto and Fujii 1998: 260). To keep the light rail system running even though it had quite severely damaged sections, shuttle buses were commissioned to transfer patrons to stations around damaged sections (Kitamura, Yamamoto and Fujii1998:256).

Other effects:

Economic impacts:

The earthquake caused approximately ten trillion yen or $102.5 billion in damage, 1.5% of Japan's GDP at the time. It is listed in the Guinness Book of records as the "costliest natural disaster to befall any one country." Most of the losses were uninsured, as only 3% of property in Kobe area was covered by earthquake insurance, compared to 16% in Tokyo. Kobe was one of the world's busiest ports prior to the earthquake, but despite the repair and rebuilding, it has never regained its former status as Japan's principal shipping port.

It was the sheer size of the earthquake caused a major decline in the Japanese stock markets, with the Nikkei 225 index plunging by a thousand points in one day following the quake. This financial damage was the immediate cause for collapse of Barings Bank due to the action of Nick Leeson, who had speculated vast amounts of money on Japanese and Singaporean derivatives. Discussions of Japan's "Lost Decade" tend towards purely economic analysis and neglect the impact of the earthquake on the Japanese economy which at the time was already suffering from recession.

The earthquake and volunteerism:

The fact that volunteers from all over Japan converged on Kobe to help victims of the quake was an important event in the history of volunteerism in Japan. The year 1995 is often regarded as a turning point in the emergence of volunteerism as a major form of civic engagement.

In December 1995, the government declared January 17 a national

"Disaster and Prevention and Volunteerism Day", and the week from January 15 to 21 a national "Disaster Prevention and Volunteerism Week", to be commemorated with lectures, seminars, and other events designed to encourage voluntary disaster preparedness and relief effort.

Effect on disaster prevention planning:

The earthquake proved to be a major wake-up call for Japanese disaster prevention authorities. Japan installed rubber blocks under bridges to absorb the shocks and rebuilt buildings further apart to prevent them falling like dominoes. The national government changed its disaster response policies in the wake of the earthquake, and its response to the 204 Chuetsu earthquakes was significantly faster and more effective. The Ground Self-Defense Forces were given automatic authority to respond to earthquakes over a certain magnitude, which allowed them to deploy to the Niigata region within minutes. Control over fire response was likewise handed over from the local fire department to a central command base in Tokyo and Kyoto.

In response to the widespread damage to transportation infrastructure, and the resulting effect on emergency response times in the disaster area, the Ministry of Land, Infrastructure and Transportation began designating special disaster prevention routes and reinforcing the roads and surrounding buildings so as to keep them as intact as possible in the event of another earthquake. Hyogo's prefecture government invested millions of yens in the years following the quake to build earthquake-proof shelters and supplies in public parks.

Elsewhere in Japan, the Tokyo metropolitan government had set up emergency food and water supply network based around petrol stations, which were mostly unaffected in the Hanshin earthquake. However, citizens' group have taken up the bulk of disaster planning partly out of distrust for the government still held after the disaster in Kobe.

Memorials:

The Kobe Luminarie, a small city of Christmas lights, is set up in the middle of Kobe City, as well as near Shin-Kobe Station every December in commemoration of the earthquake. Large "1.17" digits are illuminated at Higashi Yuenchi Park next to Kobe City Hall on January 17 of each year.

Name:

Outside Japan, the earthquake is commonly known as Kobe earthquake.

In Japanese, the disaster by this earthquake is official called. (The Great Hanshin-Awaji Earthquake Disaster Hanshin-Awaji Daishinsai), which is often shortened to The Great Hanshin Earthquake Disaster Hanshin Daishinsai).Hanshin means the region between Osaka and Kobe.

In the scientific literature is is called 7 (1995)1995 Southern Hyogo Prefecture. Earthquake Heisi 7 nen – 1995 nen-Hyogo-ken Nanbu), the name by Japan Meteorological Agency in the week after the main shock.

Mechanism of the earthquake:

Most of the largest earthquakes in Japan are caused by subduction of the Philippine Sea Plate or Pacific, with mechanism that involve either energy released within the subduction plate or the accumulation and sudden release of stress in the overlying plate. Earthquakes of these types are especially frequent in the coastal regions of northeastern Japan.

The Great Hanshin earthquake belonged to a third type, called an "inland and shallow earthquake". Earthquakes of this type occur along active faults. Even at lower magnitudes, they can be very destructive because they often occur near populated areas and because their hypocenters are located less than 20 km below the surface. The Great Hanshin earthquake began north of the island of Awaji, which lies just south of Kobe. It spread toward the southwest along the Nojima fault on Awaji and toward the northeast along the suma and Suwayama fault, which run through the center of Kobe. Observations of deformations in these faults suggest that the area was subjected to east-west compression, which is consistent with previously known crucial movements. Like earthquakes recorded in western Japan between 1891 and 1948, the 1995 earthquake had a strike-slip mechanism that accommodated east-west shorting of the Eurasian plate due to its collision with the North American plate in central Honshu.

CHAPTER TWO

As I gazed at channel CNN, I could not believe what I was looking at. It seemed as it was a dreadful movie. Then I came to my senses and realized that Japan was under attack again. It was like if the atom bombs had dropped again on Japan by the U.S. in the year 1944, but after I came to my senses, I realized that wasn't the case. I realized that it was an earthquake. The earthquake had come when the people had lest expected and in the most dreadful way, an earthquake and after a tsunami that would bring some of the people in the small towns down to their feet. It was Friday the 11th of March 2011 at 2:34 p.m., and now they would have to have help from different countries, but the Japanese people were a proud people and they didn't want to accept help from other countries, but in this dreadful case they would be compelled to have help, for food and water and medical supplies. The earthquake caught everyone by surprise and there was very little space to run and hide when the earth started shaking their land. Their worst enemy had come back to haunt them, and the residents had no idea what was happening, even though they were accustomed to earthquakes and tsunamis. Their very lives were in their hands and no one was there to save them from the worst disaster, ever, at an 8.9 earthquake. It happened quickly and it caught every one by surprise. They were stunned when the buildings started shaking. When the building started shaking, they didn't know whether to run, or hide or sit under a table for safety. It was all left to common sense of the people who were under siege. Their bad luck was happening again to them, as it seemed the Gods were not at their sides to comfort them, in their hour of need.

An hour before in Sendai, the Asano three children had come home early from school that Friday afternoon in their apartment. Asano Sayoko is the eldest daughter who is 11-years-of-age. She is a smart young lady and she sees things, hear things and most of all, she feels things. She is the guide for her family. Her sister is Asano Aiko who is 8 years-of-age and she depends upon her sister for information and help in her life. Her brother is Asano Teruo and he is nine-years-of-age. He loves his two sisters and, and he feels he is the man of the house and he likes to take care of them, but in other words this time they would have to take care of him. He has no idea what is going to confront him and his family. It is going to be the worst day of their lives.

The father of this family is Asano Hiko, who is head of the family and he is 32-years-of-age. He is a clerk in one of the banks in the city. His wife is Asano Yoko who is the mother of the three children and she is 31 years-of-age and she works in a clothing store in the city.

Asano Sayoko is a very suspicious young lady and she felt something in her bones and it was just 2:00 p.m. She kept looking up at the ceiling as if she expected the ceiling to fall on them, but in other words she knew that something dreadful was about to happen and she had a great feeling what was going to happen.

"Why are you looking up at the ceiling, Sayoko?" her bother Aiko asked suspiciously. He knew his sister Sayoko was a special person and what she was feeling was something dreadful, but he had no idea what it was. He felt in time she would tell him, and he would have to act upon her feelings.

"I feel something is about to happen, Teruo," she told him.

"What do you feel?" Aiko asked.

"I don't know," she said and she shook her head in despair. Then Sayoko went over to the phone and she called her mother at the store.

"Mama, Sayoko. You must come home now."

"Why must I come home now, Sayoko?" Asano Yoko asked curiously.

"I can feel an earthquake is coming. I can feel it. Please come home. We want you here, Mama," Sayoko pleaded, but she knew her mother wouldn't believe her, and she knew she would have to do much more convincing to her mother.

"Do as Sayoko is saying. She knows what she is saying, Mama," Teruo told his mother. He knew he had to convince his mother of what was going to happen, and it wasn't good. They needed both of their parents at home and at a time they all would need each other.

"Okay, I'll come home now and I call Papa." Yoko called her husband at the bank and she told him what Sayoko told her. "I'll come home right away," Hiko said.

Yoko went to her boss and told him she had to go home because there was an earthquake coming.

"What earthquake are you talking about?" he asked curiously. The day outside was still bright and sunny, and he didn't think of any earthquake that was coming.

"My daughter told me so on the phone, and she is right, Sir," Yoko explained.

"How do you know there is an earthquake, Sayoko?" Teruo asked.

"I can feel it in my bones and I can feel the shaking of the buildings all around us," she told him quickly. Sayoko was only able to feel that because she was a gifted child and a special child. She had to use her special abilities to take care of her family and that was because she loved them that much. She had to be there for them.

"It is a good thing we were able to tell Mama and Papa," Teruo stated. But he was still thinking of how his sister knew the earthquake was coming, and he couldn't figure it out. He was at a lost for getting it right, but he was grateful to his sister, Sayoko. She was the one who was making all the decisions.

"Now we'll just have to hope and pray. I can't afford to lose my parents. The last earthquake we lost grandfather and grandmother. We were just little at that time," Sayoko said.

"I wish they were here," Sayoko said. "We'll be in trouble shortly."

"What trouble, Sayoko?" Aiko asked.

Sayoko shook her head because she knew what was going to happen, and her sister didn't have a clue. She knew something terrible was going to happen.

"Well, tell me, Sayoko?" Aiko asked curiously.

Sayoko shook her head and she went to the window of the apartment, as if she was looking for what was going to happen shortly. Aiko went and held her sister's hand because she felt it was serious, and what was going to happen was out there, and she would need all the love her sister could give to her.

"It is out there, Aiko," Sayoko told her.

"Yes, I see. We are in trouble. Our trouble is out there," Aiko stated.

"You mean the weather, Sayoko?" Aiko asked.

"To tell you the truth, Aiko, it is worse than the weather."

"What is it?"

Sayoko swung her body from side to side as she knew her sister would understand. She didn't want to tell her in actual words. She just wanted to demonstrate her feelings to her sister.

"Yes, I understand, Sayoko. That will be an earthquake," Aiko stated. She understood what her sister was trying her best to tell her.

"Yes, Aiko, and mom and dad are not here to comfort us."

"They are at work," Aiko told her sister.

Their brother Teruo came into the room and he wanted to know what his sisters were doing. "What are you girls talking about?" he asked.

"It is like this, Teruo, Sayoko started to swing from side to side. You mean we are going to have another earthquake?" Aiko asked.

"Yes, Aiko," Teruo told her.

"Are you sure, Teruo?"

"Yes, Aiko, and mom and dad are not here as yet, so they can take care of my two beautiful sisters, Sayoko and Aiko," Teruo told them.

"And who will take care of you, Teruo?" Sayoko asked.

By this time Yoko went to her boss and told him she had to go home because an earthquake that was coming shortly.

"What earthquake?" her boss asked bluntly because he knew the day was bright and he didn't think there was an earthquake coming.

"My daughter Sayoko told me it is coming," she told him and left the store. She phoned her husband from her cell phone and told him what Sayoko told her and she ran down the street to get her bus. She wanted to hurry home now. She wanted to be there with her children. Hiko knew immediately that he had to obey his wife and get out of the bank and get home. He told his boss that he was leaving early because of an earthquake.

His boss smiled at him because he thought that Hiko was joking, but Hiko was serious. Hiko ran out of the bank quickly and he joined his bus on the road. He really wanted to get home to his children, because he loved them that much. He jump on to the bus and he was shaking like a leaf. The bus driver saw how nervous Hiko was.

"Why are you so nervous?" the bus driver asked curiously.

"I'm nervous because an earthquake is coming upon us. I want to get home to my children," Hiko told him quickly, and took his seat in the bus.

"Earthquake?" the bus driver said with a smug smile, as it was still bright outside.

When Hiko reached his destination, he jump off the bus and ran toward his building, and upstairs he went into the elevator to the six floors, and to his apartment.

Yoko traveled on the bus and when she reached where she was going, she jump off the bus and made her way to their apartment. She wished that her husband was there to look after the three kids. They needed their parents at that time, when the earthquake was shortly on their hands.

Sayoko knew what was going to happen. She was a gifted child. She saw things. She felt things and most of all she could see things and also feel things. She was a special/special child.

Sayoko went next door to her neighbor and she told her come into their apartment. Her neighbor Remi didn't know what to think. She was 65-years-of-age.

"Sayoko, why are you taking me to your apartment?" Remi asked curiously.

"Na Na, I have to take you to our apartment, because there is going to be an earthquake," Sayoko told her.

"How do you know that, Sayoko?" Remi asked curiously.

"I can feel it in my bones."

"I better call my daughter and tell her this. She should be with me," Remi said.

"Yes. You better," Sayoko said and took Remi to her apartment, so they could take care of her. Sayoko felt Remi was just like her grandmother and she had to look after her.

Sayoko called her daughter Nomi and she told her to come home because the worse is yet to come. There was going to be an earthquake shortly and her mother, Na Na was worried about her.

Aiko and Teruo just gazed at their sister and Remi was doing such a good job.

When their mother Yoko arrived in the apartment, her husband was waiting for her. They fell into each other's arms and they were happy they were there to comfort their three children and Remi.

Asano Hiko, the father went to the window to have peep and what he saw made his heart run a little faster. He saw what was happening below and he could feel the building shaking. He saw pieces of the building falling below. He shook his head and his wife Yoko knew there was trouble outside. They had got in just in time from the danger below.

Asano Hiko was 32-years-of-age and he was a clerk in a bank and he was the father of three children. Asano Yoko was 31-years-of-age, tall, slim and his beautiful wife, and she wanted them to be safe. She remembered the last earthquake in 1995, when several persons died and also some of her family. She was sure that the same thing was going to happen now. She could feel it in her bones. She knew her daughter could feel it too as she did. She was a very special person.

Sayoko was her beautiful daughter, 11-years-of-age, tall, slim and a beautiful young lady, who wanted to do wonderful things for people. Her son Teruo was 9-years-of-age, tall slim, and her second daughter, 8-years-od-age, and she was fairly tall, slim and very smart. She loved both of her parents.

The Tohoku Chiho Taiheiyo – Oki Jishim, literally. "Tohoki region. Pacific Ocean off shore earthquake". Was a 9.0 earthquake that occurred in Japan at 14.46 jst (05:', 46 UTC) on Friday 11th of March 2011.

The epicenter was reported to be 130 kilometers (81 mi) off the east coast of the Oshika Peninsula, Tohoku, with the hypocenter at a depth of 32 km (20 mi).

Hiko couldn't believe his eyes at the moment of time he saw what was happening and his apartment started shaking and what he saw below made him sick. He saw the sides of the building in front of him started falling onto the people below and screams could be heard down below of the people who were running for their lives. They knew it was an earthquake and they were running for cover.

Yoko went to the window and stood there with her husband and she knew what was happening and tears came to her eyes.

"I'm glad we are not down there. We are here with our family and Remi our neighbor, and I pray for all those people down below and many more will die before this day is ended and the earthquake is having its revenge. We are being punished all the time and we have to help ourselves," Yoko subbed.

"We'll make it, Yoko. The Gods are on our side," Hiko declared.

Nomi, that afternoon, went over to her neighbor's apartment. She felt that the Asano family were just like her family and they really took care of her that afternoon, and she was grateful for all the help, because her daughter, Norika Fujiwara and her son-in-law Aiko Fujiwara were still at work and she wanted them to come home and be safe from the earthquake. She had phoned her daughter at work and she told her she was at the Asano apartment, and she should come home, because of an earthquake on the island, but her daughter didn't believe her, because the day was still bright and sunny.

Nomi turned to Sayoko. "Please take me to your apartment. I want to see my daughter and son-in-law." Sayoko who was just nine years of age held Nomi by the hand and took her over to their apartment.

"You want to see your daughter, Na, Na?" Sayoko asked.

"Yes, Child. You are my favorite."

"Thank you, Na Na."

There were tears in Nomi's eyes. Her daughter and son-in-law were not in their apartment and she was afraid that something dreadful had happened to her beloved family, her daughter and son-in-law. She would phone her daughter and tell her to come home. She really wanted them to be with her because she was old and gray.

"No. No, Na, Na. They are still alive. You come and stay with us, Na, Na. Sayoko took Nomi back to their apartment.

When Remi and Sayoko arrived back in their apartment, Yoko made tea and sandwiches. Yoko saw the expression on Nomi's face and she knew what happened, and she felt that she and her husband would have to go and look for Nomi's daughter. They would go to her place of work and they would try to find her son-in-law.

"You can stay with us, Na, Na. We'll help you," Yoko told her.

The next day Yoko and her husband Hiko visited the place where Nomi Noroko daughter worked, but the building was in pieces. They went into the rubble, but they didn't find anyone. They didn't know what to expect. They asked around, but no one could tell them anything. They went to the hospital where Noroko's husband worked as a technician, and they found him in a ward. He was hit over the head when he was searching for his wife Noroko. She was washed away from the tsunami.

When Yoko and Hiko went home, they met their daughter, Sayoko. "Mama, what is the news? Sayoko asked.

"Not good, Child." Yoko told her.

Nomi met them in the living room and she saw the expression on their faces, and she knew what the outcome was. It was bad.

"Na, Na, we found your son-in-law Ayako. He's in the hospital. He got hit on the head," Yoko told her.

"Where is my daughter, Noroko?" Nomi asked, but she knew what the answer would be.

"We couldn't find her. The whole building was destroyed," Hiko told her."

Nomi had tears in her eyes and she sat down on the sofa. She had to think, because her beloved daughter was no more.

"Na, Na, we'll look after you. You are our great Mom," Sayoko told her and went and sat beside her.

"Thank you, Child. You are all my family," Nomi subbed.

It was a week after an old man came to the door, Yoko's door.

"My name is Yamamoto Kanji. I want to inform you that Noroko Fujiwara was found and she was unconscious and she was taken to hospital. She's okay now. She wanted me to come and tell you that," Yamamoto said and he went.

"Thank you, Mr. Yamamoto," Yoko shouted after him.

Yoko told Nomi of the good news and Nomi held her in her arms. Her daughter and son-in-law would be back in the apartment very soon, Nomi thought.

CHAPTER THREE

No one knew what would happen after the 9.0 earthquake strike Japan on the 11th of March 2011. No one was expecting what would happen after. It was seen that the worst disaster was yet to come, and it only took a few minutes to arrive on land from the sea. The great tsunami was at its best, waving and swinging from side to side as if it was, crazy. The high wall with a gate which would prevent water from coming into the towns, and villages, did not close the gate, and the head fire chief had to send three of his men to close that gate manually, but time wasn't on their side, and the 20 foot wave of tsunami wave came from the sea quickly. The fire chief from a distance watched in horror and he knew what was going to happen, as he saw the high 20 foot wave went over the wall, and the water went straight over his three men, and he knew at that moment of time that they would be no more. He had sacrificed his three men to close the gate. The water was swift and powerful and it took everything in its path, people, houses, cars and anything else. It was now a moment of climax for all the people in that town. They had no idea that their lives would end in this dreadful way by a sea of water. It was really a death sentence. The fire chief cried when he saw what had happened to his men, and he wished at that moment of time that the tsunami had taken him instead, but he was still alive, and he had to face the force in front of him, and carry out his duties accordingly. He was supposed to be brave, but at that moment of time he was really weak and helpless to any one, but he had to pull himself together and get to work. His life was now on the edge.

The great tsunami had made its mark and washed the whole town and everything in it inward and outward it rolled back into the sea after doing all of its damage and taking the lives of the whole town. No one believed it was such a great tsunami, doing all that damage and going out to sea again. It was an awful sight to see, and those who saw it would remember it for the rest of their lives.

After the tsunami struck one village, the village vanished into thin air. When the earthquake had struck several minutes later, the great ocean turned. The ocean swelled and made a wall of over 20 foot up, making its way onto the village, Satton, Japan. It rolled onto land as if it were mad. It was hard to believe that there was a village there after the tsunami hit shore and did its great damage with a vengeance.

It was the great tsunami that devastated Japan's coast as the tsunami rolled through it as if it were a tree-lined ocean cove and obliterated nearly everything in its path in this village of about 250 people and 70 houses, which were washed away like paper chips. The people of the village had no chance as their precious lives were taken from them, and they were no more.

Now, three days later in Satton that glimpse into the phenomenal destruction caused by this killer wave that followed Japan's most powerful earthquake on record, and one of the five strongest earthquakes on earth in the past 110 years ago. No one expected the same earthquake would attack them again – the same meant the strongest.

In Satton and nearby areas, there was no electricity to give the people power, no running water. There were no generators humming to give the people power. It was the four generators that had crashed in Fukushima, leaving just two to run the city, and that was not a good cause. It was bad and no one would predict the outcome. That night was pitched black. The buildings that were still standing were closed. No stores were open. Everything had stopped. It was the end of a dreadful day, where people were suffering.

No one knew the earthquake would trigger such a large tsunami after the quake. This tsunami would cause so much damage to towns and villages. The gate and the walls that would prevented much sea water from coming to shore. The gate was supposed to close automatically, but it didn't and the chief fireman had to send out three of his subordinates to close the gate, and he watched the whole procedure from high above, and what he saw made his skin crawl. He saw the large wave coming swiftly to shore and he knew his men were in the way, and he knew immediately that he had sacrificed them to close the gate, and they were no match for the 20 foot wall of sea water that went over them, and the tsunami was so fast that it took the firemen away, and their lives were no more. The tsunami made its way to the people of the village and the giant wave was killing them as they met. Some of the people were saved by a miracle. One man and his wife went on top of their house and the large wave went to them inside the village, and then out to sea, and only the woman's husband was saved and his wife was washed away at sea, but it was his destiny to be alive. The man was picked up after two days at sea on top of his house. He was really fortunate to be alive. It was his destiny.

It was the tsunami warning in Sendai and the evacuations along the Japan's Pacific coast and in at least 20 countries, including the entire Pacific coast of North America and South America. The earthquake created extremely destructive tsunami waves up to 10 meters high (33 ft) that struck Japan minutes after the quake, and in some cases traveling up to 10 km (6 ml) inland, with smaller waves after several hours in many other countries.

The large wave had taken away, cars, people and buildings, and the whole village of Satton, and the whole village was lost and every one who was left alive was left in a trance.

When the tsunami hit on the north side of the coast – it hit the schools and children were still in the schools learning their lessons. The poor little kids didn't know what hit them. They were unfortunate and they didn't stand a chance and it would seem that the Gods were on their side. They died in vane and there was no one to save them. The large wave had taken their lives.

Their mothers knew what the tsunami had done to their kids, weep, their kids were gone whom they brought on this earth, and they were shocked when their kids were all gone. Their cries and screams they thought would make the bad things go away.

The tsunami had washed away the whole town and also washed the people away – their lives were gone forever. No one was safe from the tsunami – the tsunami is the devil's will, causing nearly two billion in damages.

"There was nothing left," villager Toshio Abe told The Associated Press on Monday as firefighters in bright orange and yellow emergency suits hacked through the vast wasteland with pickaxes, searching not for survivors but for the dead. Abe said at least 40 of Satton's people were dead or unaccounted for. The great tsunami had taken them away into the sea. It wasn't really their day to live.

Abe said he was gardening on Friday afternoon when he felt the earthquake under his feet. Tsunami sirens blared and a loudspeaker announcement warned people to get to higher ground, but this was too late – the earthquake and they the tsunami came quickly and no one had the chance to get to higher ground, and some of them would be sacrificed.

The 70-year-old frantically knew what he had to do and he quickly climbed a hill behind his home above two kilometers, or roughly a mile from the beach. From his safe vantage point, he watched as, 20 or 30 minutes later, the giant wave arrived with a thunderous roar. He was really glad that he made it up to safety, but he felt sad because of all of his friends below didn't take the warning seriously, and their lives would be in peril.

The large wave came with a roar and it crashed through what appeared to be a two-story-high sea gate, and then it careened through the valley, following a two-lane road. He saw it rise up, over and through a bridge and smash into scores of houses, ripping most apart instantly. Other houses, he said, were pulled from their foundations and slammed together. The large wave was doing its best at that, ripping everything in its path.

It were hills on both sides of that channeled the wave another kilometer or so inland, depositing the broken innards of Satton's homes along the road. No homes were safe and all homes in its path were wrecked and taken away at sea.

"I never thought the tsunami would have come so far inland," Abe said. "I thought we were safe, but the tsunami had to do its work."

Abe pointed to a battered concrete foundation amid the flattened landscape. It was his house. "I will rebuild," he said, "but not here."

"That was city hall," said 48-old construction worker Takama Oyama, gesturing toward a two-story white building that stood alone near the beach, leaning at an angle into a sheet of mud and sand. Every one was looking at the things they loved and was gone. It was really a shock to them, an unbelievable shock to them.

"That was our elementary school," he said, pointing to a three-story building a few hundred yards away whose entire façade had been ripped off and was covered in black and yellow ocean buoys. Most everything else has disappeared, and the children were sacrificed in the school by the tsunami.

"We struggled, but it is all gone," Oyama said. "Everything is lost."

Behind him, a tranquil tree-covered the island could be seen just off the coast. That such violence could come from such a picturesque view seemed contradictory, hard to believe.

One crumpled sign indicated there had once been a train station here, a fact Abe confirmed. It was hard to tell where, though. There were no tracks, no trains, no station.

Crushed bulldozers had been turned upside down. The blue-tiled roof of one house lay across a bridge. The wheels of a vehicle stuck from under the roof.

A few yards away, a bloated black-spotted white cow lay on the foundation of another vanished home, streams of dried blood running from its pink nose and its eyes looking over the destruction. Embedded in the hardened silt nearby lay a blue stroller and it was covered in what looked like hay.

"We can never live here again," Oyama said as he rested with his wife on a concrete ledge of the broken tarmac road. During an interview, the ledge tremble as another aftershock hit the region.

Oyama, was asked how many people died, Oyama shrugged. "We've only seen a few bodies," he said. "I think everybody was swept out to sea."

In the wide region of Minamisanrikucho, of which Satton is just one costal village. Abe cited authorities as saying at least 4,500 of the 17,000 inhabitants were believed dead. Police estimated 10,000 dead among the 2.3 million people in the Miyagi prefecture, the Japanese equivalent of a state.

The firefighters who arrived Monday came from inland town to pick through the rubble. They were wearing goggles and dust masks and they carried long pickaxes, chainsaw and backpacks. They looked like spacemen walking across a gigantic lunar garbage dump. They had no idea of what they would find because no body was left alive.

As a Japanese self-defense force helicopter circled overhead, they lifted one hunched and frozen corpse from the mud of a dried canal filled with smashed cars and twisted mountains of corrugated iron sheeting. The tsunami had pulled the dead man's dark blue plaid shirt over his head. His white knuckles were visible, and his hand was still clenched.

The firefighters covered him in a blue plastic tap and carried him away on a stretcher. Later, they found another corpse in the rubble and carted that one away, too.

Their job was to find all those who met their untimely death and bury them.

The road that winds through Satton was broken apart in several spots. At one point – where the tsunami wave stopped – it went into a quiet neighborhood of another village where two-story houses were standing perfectly intact, and their windows not even shattered, as if nothing ever happened. They were lucky at this time that the tsunami had missed their houses and they had come out of a bad situation safely. It seems as if the Gods were on their side.

There, on the pavement, in front of a small government house-turned shelter where survivors rested on tatami mats and somebody had scrawled huge white letters in the road for air crews to see SOS. They wanted people to know that the road was damaged and vehicles would not be able to drive through on the road. The residents knew that they couldn't drive through on that road, and now they had to use their legs. They had to walk to where they wanted to get to and they had to view the terrible sites in front of them or at their left and right sides of the road.

CHAPTER FOUR

Japan earthquake caused nuke trouble, triggering evacuation of 3K residents:

Japan's massive earthquake caused a power outage that disabled a nuclear reactor's cooling system, triggering evacuation orders for about 3,000 residents as the government declared its first-ever state emergency at a nuclear plant. The people in that area knew that it would be trouble and health problems if they stayed, and their health was important. The nuclear plant was a killer by itself and radiation would kill all those people who were near the nuclear plant.

Japan's nuclear safety agency said pressure inside one of the six boiling water reactors at the Fukushima Daiichi plant had risen to 1.5 times the level, which was dangerous to the health of the residents.

Natalia Jimenez:

An aerial short shows vehicles that were ready for shipping, was being carried away by Tsunami tidal wave at Hitachinaka city in Ibaraki Prefacture on March 11, 2011, a massive 8.8 – magnitude earthquake shook Japan unleashing a powerful tsunami that sent ships crashing into shores, and carried cars through the streets of costal towns like feathers.

It was considered normal hours after the evacuation order that the government announced that the plant in northeastern Japan will release slightly more radioactive vapor from the unit to lower the pressure in an effort to protect it from possible meltdown. This was bad news for the residents in that area.

The Chief Cabinet Secretary Yukio Edano said the amount of

radioactive element in the vapor was "very small" and would not affect the environment or human health. "With evacuation in place and the ocean-bound wind, we can ensure the safety," he said at a televised news conference early Saturday.

After the quake triggered a power outage, a backup generator also failed and the cooling system was unable to supply water to cool the 460-megawatt No. 1 reactor, and though at least one backup cooling system was being used. The reactor core remained hot even after a shutdown. The workers at the power plant knew that there was great danger there, and they were trying their best to fix the problem, but little did they know the whole situation was worse than they thought.

The agency said plant workers were scrambling to restore cooling water supply at the plant, but there was no prospect for an immediate success. Their efforts were in vain.

Edano said the 40-year-old plant was not leaking radiation. The plant was in Onahama City, about 170 miles (270 kilometers) northeast of Tokyo. The situation at that moment of time was getting serious, and all precaution was taken to get citizens outside that area.

If the outage in the cooling system persisted, eventually radiation could leak out into the environment and in the worst possible way and it could cause a reactor to meltdown, a nuclear safety agency official said on condition of anonymity and citing sensitivity of the issue. He knew the situation was in real danger.

Another official at the nuclear agency, Yuji Kakizaki, said that plant workers were cooling the reactor with a secondary cooling system, which was not as effective at the regular cooling method. It was presumed that they were cooling the reactor with sea water, the next best thing.

Kakizaki said officials have confirmed that the emergency cooling system – the last ditch cooling measure to prevent the reactor from the meltdown – is intact and could kick in if needed, but that at the moment was quite misleading.

"That's as a last resort, and we have not reached that stage yet," Kakizaki added.

Japan's nuclear safety agency said the evacuation, ordered by the local government of Fukushima, affects at least 2,800 people. Edano said residents were told to stay at least two miles (three kilometers) from the plant and stay inside buildings.

He said it was the state of emergency and evacuation order was for precautionary measures.

"We launched the measure so can be fully prepared for the worst scenario," he said. "We are using all our might to deal with the situation."

Defense Ministry official Ippo Maeyama said the ministry has dispatched dozens of troops trained for chemical disasters to the Fukushima plant in case of a radiation leak, along with four vehicles designed for use in atomic, biological and chemical warfare.

Pineville, La., resident Janie Eudy said her husband, Danny, was working at Fukushima No. 1 when the earthquake stuck. After a harrowing evacuation, he called her several hours later from the parking lot of his quake-ravaged hotel.

He and another American plant worker were "waiting to be rescued, and they were in bad shape," she said in a telephone interview.

Danny Eudy, 52, a technician employed by Pasadena, Texas-based Atlantic Plant Maintenance, told his wife the quake violently shook the plant building he was in.

Eudy told his wife that he and other workers were evacuating the plant when the tsunami swept through the area, carrying away homes and vehicles. They retreated so they wouldn't get caught up in the raging water.

"He walked through so much glass that his feet were cut, and that slowed him down," she said. His feet were cut and he didn't feel anything, because the situation was so dangerous, and one's life depended upon their safety.

After the water started to recede, Eudy and other workers drove to their hotel, and only to find it in shambles.

"Most of the hotel was gone," she said. "He said the roads were torn up and everything was a mess."

His hotel room was demolished along with all of his belongings, so Eudy had to borrow a resident's phone to call his wife early that morning. The workers were waiting for daylight, but contemplating seeking higher ground in case another big wave hit.

"He sounded like he was in shock. He was scared," Janie Eudy said. "They are totally on their own, trying to just make it."

Neil Sheehan, a spokesman for the U.S. Nuclear Regulatory Commission, said staff was trying to collect more information on what was happening.

At the Fukushima Dilchi site, "They are busy trying to get coolant to the core area," Sheehan said. "The big thing is trying to get power to the cooling systems."

Speaking at the White House, Secretary of State Hilary Clinton also said U.S. Air planes were carrying "some really important coolant" to the site. She said "one of their plants came under a lot of stress with the earthquake and didn't have enough coolant."

High pressure pumps can temporarily cool a reactor in this state with battery power, even when electricity is down according to Arnold Gundersen, a nuclear engineer who used to work in the U.S. nuclear industry. Batteries would go dead within hours but could be replaced.

The nuclear reactor was among 10 in Japan shut down because of the earthquake.

The Fukushima plant is just south of the worst-hit Miyagi prefecture, where a fire broke out at another nuclear plant. The blaze was in a turbine building at one of the Onagawa power plants. Smoke could be seen coming out of the building, which is separated from the plant's reactor, Tohoku Electric Power Co. said. The fire has since been extinguished.

Another reactor at Onagawa was experiencing a water leak and that was serious. They had to find ways and means of stopping the leak before it got more serious.

The U.S. Geological Survey said the 2.46 p.m. quake was a magnitude of 8.9, the biggest earthquake to hit Japan since official began keeping records in the late 1800s.

A tsunami warning was issued for a number of Pacific, Southeast Asian and Latin American nations.

At the two-reactor Diablo Canyon plant at Avila Beach, California, an "unusual event" – the lowest level of alert – was declared in connection with a West Coast tsunami warning. The plant remained stable, through, and kept running, according to the NRC.

CHAPTER FIVE

Hundreds killed in Tsunami after 8.9 Japan Earthquake:
A ferocious tsunami unleashed by Japan's biggest recorded earthquake slammed into the eastern coast Friday 11th of March 2011, killing hundreds of people as it carried away ships, cars and homes, and it triggered widespread fires that burnt out of control.

Hours later, the waves washed ashore on Hawaii and the U.S. West coast, where evacuations were ordered from California to Washington, but little damage was reported. The entire Pacific was put on alert – including coastal areas of South America, Canada and Alaska, but waves weren't as bad as expected.

In northeastern Japan, the area around a nuclear power plant was evacuated after the reactor's cooling system failed and pressure began building inside, and this was on account of the great tsunami that hit the town, causing major damages.

The Police said 200 to 300 bodies were found in the northeastern costal city of Sendai, the city in Miyagi prefecture, or state, closed to the epicenter. But authorities said they weren't able to reach the area because of damage to the roads. The tsunami had done its best to uproot the roads, making it impossible to drive on them, and that was bad for residents.

A police official, who declined to be named because of department policy, said it may be a while before rescuers could reach the area to get a more precise body count. So far, they have confirmed 178 were killed with 584 residents missing. Police also said 947 people were injured, and needed help for medical treatment.

The magnitude 8.9 offshore quake triggered a 23-foot (seven-meter) tsunami and was followed for hours by more than 50 aftershocks, and many of them more than a magnitude of 6.0 in the early hours of Saturday, a magnitude of 6.7 earthquake struck the central, mountainous part of the country, and far from the original quake's epicenter. It was not immediately clear if this latest quake was related to the others.

Friday's massive quake shook dozens of cities and villages along a 1,300-mile (2,100-kilometer) stretch of coast, including Tokyo, hundreds of miles (kilometers) from the epicenter. A large section of Kesennuma, a town of 70,000 people in Miyagi, burned furiously into the night with no apparent hope of being extinguished by the authorities.

Koto Fujikawa, 28 residents were riding a monorail when the quake hit and had to pick her way along a narrow, elevated track to the nearest station.

"I thought I was going to die," Fujikawa, who works for a marketing company, said "It felt like the whole structure was collapsing."

Scientists said the quake ranked as the fifth-largest earthquake in the world since 1900 and was nearly 8,.000 times stronger than one that devastated Christchurch, New Zealand, last month. There was no safe place for an earthquake, as it strikes wherever it is meant to strike in any country, and no one was safe from its devastation. .

"The energy radiated by this quake was nearly equal to one month's worth of energy consumption" in the United States, US Geological Survey Scientist Brian Atwater told The Associated Press.

President Barack Obama pledged US assistance following what he called a potentially "catastrophic" disaster. He said one US aircraft carrier is already in Japan, and a second is on its way. A US ship was also heading to the Marianas islands as needed.

An American man working at one of the nuclear plants near the coast when the quake hit said whole building shook, and debris fell from the ceiling and Danny Eudy 52, a technician employed by Pasadena, Texas-based Atlantic Plant Maintenance, and his colleagues escaped the building just as the tsunami hit, his wife told The Associated Press.

The group watched homes and vehicles carried away in the wave and found their hotel mostly swept away when they finally reach it. Now they had no way to stay and they had to wait for help to come.

Even for a country used to earthquakes, this one was of horrific proportions because the tsunami that crashed ashore, swallowing everything in its path as it surged several times (kilometers) inland before retreating, and taking a large amount of stuff with it. The apocalyptic images on Japanese TV powerful, debris-filled waves, uncontrolled fires and a ship caught in a massive whirlpool resembled scenes from a Hollywood movie.

Large fishing boats and other vessels rode high waves ashore, slamming against overpasses or scraping under them and snapping power lines along the way. Upturned and partially submerged cars bobbed in the water. Ships anchored in ports crashed against each other. No one knew whether they were coming or going. The whole situation was really dangerous, and no one predict what was happening.

At least two trains were swept of the tracks along the coast, but no one was hurt, though five passengers from one train scrambled to the roof of a nearby house. He didn't want to be swept away by the tsunami, and his only break was to get on the roof top, and save his life, as his life was precious to him.

The tsunami roared over embankments, washing anything in its path inland before reversing directions and carrying cars, homes and other debris out to sea. Flames shot from some of the homes, probably because a burst gas pipe which caught fire and burned.

Waves of muddy waters flowed over farmland near Sendai, carrying some of them ablaze. Divers attempted to flee. Sendai airport was inundated with thick, muddy debris that included cars, trucks, buses and even light planes.

Highways to the worst-hit costal areas buckled. Telephone lines snapped. Train service in northeastern Japan and in Tokyo, which normally serve 10 million people a day, were suspended, leaving untold numbers of passengers stranded in stations or roaming the streets. Tokyo's Narita airport was closed indefinitely.

In one town alone on the northeastern coast, Minami-soma, some 1,800 houses were destroyed or badly ravaged, a Defense Ministry spokeswoman said.

As night fell and temperatures hovered just above freezing, tens of thousands of people remained stranded in Tokyo, where the rail network was still down. The streets were jammed with cars, buses and trucks trying to get out of the city.

The city set up 33 shelters in city hall, on university campuses and government offices, but many planned to spend the night at 24-hour cafes, hotels and offices.

Japanese automakers Toyoto, Nissan and Honda halted production at some assembly plants in areas hit by the quake. One worker was killed and more than 30 injured after being crushed by a collapsing wall at a Honda Motor Co. research facility in northeastern Tochigi prefecture, the company said.

Jessie Johnson, a native of the U.S. state of Nevada who lives in Chiba, north of Tokyo, was eating at a sushi restaurant with his wife when the quake hit.

"At first it didn't feel unusual, but then it went on. So I got myself and my wife under the table," he said. "I've lived here for 10 years, and I've never felt anything like that before. The aftershocks keep coming. It's gotten to the point where I don't know whether it's me shaking an earthquake."

NHK said more than 4 million buildings were without power in Tokyo and its suburbs.

A large fire erupted at the Cosmo oil refinery in the city of Ichihara and burned out of control with 100-foot (30-meter) flames whipped into the sky. The earthquake had caused this fire in the refinery.

"Our initial assessment indicates that there has already been enormous damage," Chief Cabinet Secretary.

He said the Defense Ministry was sending troops to the hardest-hit region. A utility aircraft and several helicopters were on the way.

Also in Miyagi prefecture, a fire broke out in a turbine of a nuclear power plant, but it was later extinguished, said the Tohoku Power Co.

A reactor area of a nearby plant was leaking water, the company said. But it was unclear if the leak was caused by the tsunami or something else. There were no reports of radioactive leaks at any of Japan's nuclear plants.

Hiroshi Sato, a disaster management official in northern – water prefecture, said officials were having trouble getting an overall picture of the whole destruction.

"We don't even know the extent of damage. Roads were badly damaged and cut off as tsunami washed away debris, cars and many other things," he said.

The U.S. Geological Survey said the 2.46 p.m. quake was a magnitude of 8.9, the biggest to hit Japan since record-keeping in the late 1800s and one of the biggest ever recorded in the world.

The quake struck at a depth of six miles (10 kilometers), about 80 miles (125 kilometers) off the eastern coast the agency said. The area is 240 miles (380 kilometers) northeast of Tokyo. Several quakes hit the same region in recent days, including one measured at magnitude 7.3 on Wednesday that caused no damage.

A tsunami warning was extended to a number if areas in the Pacific, Southeast Asia and Latin America, including Japan, Russia, Indonesia, New Zealand and Chile. In the Philippines, authorities ordered an evacuation of costal communities, but no unusual waves were reported.

Thousands fled homes in Indonesia after officials warned of a tsunami up to 6 feet (2 meters), but waves of only 4 inches (10 centimeters) were measured. No big wave came to the Northern Mariana Islands, a US territory, either.

The first wave hit Hawaii about 9 a.m. EST (1400 GMT). A tsunami about 7 feet (2.1 meters) high was recorded on Maui and a wave at least 3 feet (a meter) high was recorded on Oahu and Kaual. Official warned that the waves would continue and could get larger.

Japan's worst previous quake was a magnitude of 8.3 temblor in 1923, in Kanto that killed 143, 000 according to USGS. A 7.2 magnitude quake in Kobe in 1995 killed 6,400 people. The Japanese people were unfortunate and it wasn't the way to die by an earthquake. Their dreams and their love were taken away by a quake.

Japan lies on the "Ring of Fire" – an arc of earthquake and volcanic zones stretching around the Pacific where about 90 percent of the world's quakes occur, including the one that triggered the December 26, 2004, Indian Ocean tsunami that killed an estimated 230,000 in 12 nations. A magnitude 8.8 temblor that shook central Chile in February 2010 also generated a tsunami and it killed 524 people.

CHAPTER SIX

Japan races to contain the nuclear threat after the quake. In this case it meant that the whole case of the nuclear was melting and some of the people of Japan, who were brave and loyal to the people of Japan had to go into the nuclear reactors. They knew that job was a death sentence, but some one had to do it and saved so many people from being affected from a nuclear threat.

It was dangerous radiation was leaking from those four reactors, and the crippled nuclear reactors and the government had to force 140,000 people to remove from the reactors because of radiation.

In a national televised statement, Prime Minister Naoto Kan said radiation had spread from the four stricken reactors of the Fukushima Daiichi nuclear plant along Japan's northeastern coast. The region in Japan was shattered on Friday by a 9.0-magnitude earthquake, and an ensuing tsunami that is believed to have killed more than 10,000 people, and plunged millions into misery, and pummeled the world's third-largest economy of Japan.

Japanese officials told the international Atomic Energy Agency that the reactor fire was in a fuel storage pond – an area where used nuclear fuel is kept cool, and that "radioactivity is being released directly into the atmosphere". Long after the fire was extinguished, a Japanese official the pool might still be boiling through the reported levels of radiation had dropped dramatically by the end of the day.

Late on Tuesday, officials at the plant said they were considering asking for help from the U.S, and the Japanese military sprayed water from helicopters into the pool.

The reactor in Fukushima Daiichi, Unit 4 had been shut down before the quake for maintenance.

If the water boils, it could evaporate, exposing the rods. The fuel rods are encased in safety to prevent them from resuming nuclear reactions, nuclear officials said. But they acknowledged that there could have been damage to the containers. They confirmed that the walls of the storage pool building were damaged.

Experts noted that much of the leaking radiation was apparently in steam from boiling water. It had been emitted directly by fuel rods, which would be far virulent, they say.

"It is not good, but I don't think it's a disaster," said Steve Crossley, an Australian based radiation physicist.

Even the highest detected rates were not automatically harmful for brief periods, he said. "If you were to spend a significant amount of time in the order of hours – that could be significant," Crossley said.

Less clear the results of the blast in Unit 2, near a suppression pool, which removes heat under a reactor vessel, said plant owner Tokyo Electric Power Co. The nuclear core was not damage but the bottom of the surrounding container may have been, said Shigekazu Omukai, a spokesman for Japan's nuclear safety agency.

Though Kan and other officials urged claim, Tuesday's developments fueled a growing panic in Japan and around the world amid widespread uncertainty over what would happen next. They knew the whole situation was getting serious by the minute.

In the worst case scenario, one or more of the reactor cores would completely melt down, a disaster that could spew large amounts of radioactivity into the atmosphere.

"I worry a lot about fallout," said Yuta Tadano, a 20-year-old pump technician at the Fukushima plant, who said he was in the complex when the quake hit.

"If we could see it, we could escape, but we can't," he said, cradling his 4-month-old baby, Shoma, at an evacuation center.

The radiation fears added to the catastrophe that has been unfolding in Japan, where at east 10,000 people are believed to have been killed, and millions of people were facing a fifth night with little food, water or heating in near-freezing temperatures and snow as they dealt with the loss of their homes and loved ones. Up to 450,000 people are in temporary shelters.

Hundreds of aftershocks have shaken Japan's northeast and Tokyo since the original offshore quake, including one on Tuesday night whose epicenter was hundreds of miles (kilometers) southwest and inland. The shocks were felt in those areas.

Officials have only been able confirm a far lower toll – about 3,300 killed – but those who were involved in the 2004 Asian tsunami said there was no question more people died and warned that, like the earlier disaster, and many thousands may never be found. Their bodies washed away at sea.

Asia's richest country hasn't seen such hardship since World War II. The stock market plunged a second day and a spate of panic buying saw stores running out of necessities, raising government fears that hoarding may hurt the delivery of emergency food aid to those who really need it.

In a rare bit of good news, rescuers found two survivors Tuesday in the rubble left by the tsunami that hit the northeast, including a 70-year-old woman whose house was tossed off its foundation. This lady was lucky to be found alive in the rubble – the Gods had spared her life, so she could tell another story at age 70.

The Fukushima Daiichi nuclear complex, along that battered coastline, has been the focus of the worries. Workers there have been desperately trying to use seawater to cool the rods in the complex's three reactors, because all of which lost their cooling ability after Friday's quake and tsunami.

Afterward, officials in Ibaraki, a neighboring prefecture just south of the area, said up to 100 times the normal level of radiation were detected Tuesday. While those figures are worrying if there are prolonged exposure, and they are far from fatal.

Tokyo reported slightly elevated radiation levels, but officials said the increase was too small to threaten the 39 million people in and around the capital, about 170 miles (270 kilometers) away.

Further south of the capital, air monitoring equipment on the aircraft carried USS George Washington detected low levels of radioactivity as it sat at Yokosuka, a US 7th Fleet spokesman said.

Comdr. Jeff Davis said there was no danger to the public. But military personnel at Yokosuka and Naval Air Facility Stsugi were advised to limit their time outside and seal ventilation systems at their homes.

Amid concerns about radiation, Austria moved its embassy from Tokyo to Osaka.

Meanwhile, Air China and China Eastern Airlines canceled flights to Tokyo and two cities in the disaster area. Germany's Lufthansa airlines were also diverting two daily flights to Tokyo to other Japanese cities. None mentioned radiation concerns, instead giving no explanation or citing the airports' limited capacities.

Closer to the stricken nuclear complex, the streets in the costal city of Soma were empty as the few residents who remained there heeded the government's warning to stay indoors.

Prime Minister Kan and others warned there is a danger of more leaks and told people living within 20 miles (30 kilometers) of the Fukushima Daiichi complex to stay indoors to avoid exposure that could make people sick,

The government also imposed a no-fly zone over that area for commercial traffic.

Some 70,000 people had always been evacuated from a 12-mile (20 kilometer) radius from the Daiichi complex. About 140,000 remain in the larger danger zone.

"Please do not go outside. Please stay indoors. Please close windows and make your homes airtight," Chief Cabinet Secretary Yuko Edano told residents in the danger zone.

"These are figures that potentially affect health. There is no mistake about that," he said.

Weather forecast for Fukushima were for snow and wind Tuesday evening, blowing southwest toward Tokyo then shifting and blowing east out to sea. That's important because it shows which direction a possible nuclear cloud might blow.

The US Navy said several helicopter crews involved in relief efforts were exposed to low levels of radiation Tuesday. Like 17 crew members exposed the previous day, and the personnel had to go through a decontamination process which can involve a simple scrub down with soap and water.

The Navy also said it was sending some of its ships to operate off the country's west coast instead of the east to avoid hazards from debris into the sea by the tsunami and to be farther away from radiation.

Officials said 70 workers were at the nuclear complex, struggling with its myriad problems. The workers all of then wearing protective gear, were being rotated in and out of the danger zone quickly to reduce their radiation exposure.

Another 800 staff were evacuated. The fires and explosions at the reactors have injured 15 workers and military personnel and exposed up to 190 people to elevated radiation.

Temperatures in at least two of the complex's units 5 and 6 were also slightly elevated, Edano said.

"The power for cooling is not working well and the temperature was gradually rising, so it was necessary to control it," he said.

Fourteen pumps have been brought into get seawater into the other reactors. They are not yet pumping water into Unit 4 but are trying to figure out how to do that.

In Tokyo, slightly higher-than normal radiation levels were detected Tuesday, but officials insisted there are no health dangers.

"The amount was extremely small and it did not raise health concerns. It will not affect us," Takayuki Fujiki, a Tokyo government official said.

Edano said the radiation readings had fallen significantly by the evening.

Japanese government officials were being rightly cautious, said Donald Clander, professor emeritus of nuclear engineering at the University of California at Berkeley. He believed even the heavily elevated levels of radiation around Daiichi was "not a health hazard". But without knowing specific levels, he said it was hard to make judgments.

"Right now it is worse than Three Mile Island." Olander said. But it is nowhere near the levels released during Chernobyl.

On Three Mile Island the radiation leak was held inside the containment shell – thick concrete armor around the reactor. The Chernobyl reactor had no shell and was also operational when the disaster struck. The Japanese reactors automatically shut down when the quake hit and are encased in containment shells.

The impact of the earthquake and tsunami dragged down stock markets. The benchmark Nikkei 225 stock average plunged for a second day Tuesday, nose-diving more than 10 percent to close at 8,605. 15 while the broader topic lost more than 8 percent.

To lessen the damage, Japan's central bank made two cash injections totaling 8 trillion yen ($98 billion) Tuesday into the money markets after pumping in $184 billion on Monday.

Initial estimates put repair cost in the tens of billions of dollars, cost that would likely add to a massive debt that, at 200 percent of gross domestic product, is the biggest among industrialized nations.

No one knew what was happening. The whole situation with the reactors, the whole situation was far worse than the government was telling them. It was like a hide and seek situation. The government knew they had to give false information, as they didn't want the people to get all worked up over radiation. The Japanese people were proud and strong and they knew where the situation lay, and they had to go along with it. They couldn't let something like that get them down – they were strong and they had to fight for a good outcome to come. The people couldn't know the real truth to this dreadful situation.

The government knew they needed help badly this time because they had no idea how to rectify the whole situation. They needed help from the U.S. and the U.S. could be their savor. They had never asked for help like this before, but now it was essential, and may be the whole situation could be fixed, but they knew it was just a dream – a dream that mat be would come true, and the people of Japan would be saved, where they would be in a position to up lift their families, and grow new ones in the midst.

The cost of rebuilding the whole country – the money would be coming from several different countries – it would be in the cost of two hundred billion dollars for them to fulfill their city to the original position. It is their island and there they were meant to live and there they were meant to die.

CHAPTER SEVEN

Tide of bodies overwhelms quake – hit Japan:
 Tagajo, Japan – A tide of bodies washed up along Japan's coastline on Monday, and it was overwhelming cremations, and exhausting supplies of body bags had to be available, and adding to the spiraling humanitarian, economic and nuclear crisis after the massive earthquake and tsunami. The tsunami had taken the bodies out at sea and now the tide was washing the bodies back on shore. This was a terrible site for the workers of the city. Their job was now to pick up the pieces and cremate the dead. It was really a sad situation for them to handle, but that was their real task, and it would be a task they would never forget.
 Millions of people were facing a fourth night without water, food or heating in near-freezing temperatures along the northeast coast that was devastated by Friday's disasters. Meanwhile, a third reactor at a nuclear power plant in Fukushima lost its cooling capacity and its fuel rods were fully exposed, and it was raising fears of a meltdown, and that was bad news for the residents of the area.
 The stock market plunged over the likelihood of huge losses by Japan industries, including big names such as Toyoto and Honda. It is assumed that when the tsunami came ashore, unfortunately it washed all the new cars from the factory which were parked outside and washed them into the sea, and that was a great lost for each factory in that area.
 On the coastline of Miyagi prefecture, which took the full force of the tsunami, a Japanese police official said 1,000 bodies were found scattered across the coastline. Kypdo, the Japanese news agency reported that 2,000

bodies washed up on shorelines in Miyagi. It was a rush to bag off all those bodies, and to make a place for burial.

In one town in a neighborhood prefecture, the crematorium was unable to handle that large number of bodies being brought in for funerals.

"We have already begun cremations, but we can only handle 18 bodies a day. We are overwhelmed and are asking other cities to help us deal with bodies. We only have one crematorium in town," Katsuhiko Abe, an official in Soma, said.

While the official death toll rose to nearly 1,900, the discovery of the washed-up bodies and other reports of deaths suggested the true number was much higher in Miyagi, and the police chief has said 10,000 people are estimated to have died in his province alone. They didn't make any plans for so many bodies that washed ashore and they knew they had to make other plans to get rid of the bodies and quickly.

The outspoken governor of Tokyo, Shintaro Ishihara, told reporters Monday that the disaster was "punishment from heaven" because Japanese have become greedy. But little did he know he was right on that aspect. The Gods were punishing the people of Japan, making their world a miserably one.

Across Japan, most people opt to cremate their dead. With so many bodies, the government on Monday waved a rule requiring permission first from local authorities before cremation on burial to speed up funerals, said Health Ministry official Yukio Okuda. That was a most import situation and they had to make more proper arrangements, so as to take of their dead in a proper way.

"The current situation was so extraordinary, and it was very likely that crematoriums were running beyond capacity," said Okuda. "This is an emergency measure. We want to help quake hit people as much as we can."

Friday's double tragedy has caused unimaginable deprivation of people of this industrialized country – Asia's richest – which hasn't seen hardship since World War II. In many areas there was no running water, and no power and four to five-hour waits for gasoline. People were suppressing hunger with instant noodles or rice balls while dealing with the loss of loved ones and homes.

"People were surviving on the food and water. Things were simply not coming," said Hajime Sato, a government official in Iwate prefecture, and one of the hardest hit areas.

Sato said deliveries of food and other supplies were just 10 percent of what was needed. Body bags and coffins were running so short that the government may turn to foreign funeral homes for help, he said.

"We have requested funeral homes across the nation to send us many bags and coffins. But we simply don't have enough," he said. "We just did not expect such a dreadful thing to happen. It's just overwhelming."

The pulverized coast has been hit by hundreds of aftershocks since the latest one. It was a 6.2 magnitude quake that was followed by a new tsunami scare Monday.

As sirens wailed soldiers abandoned their search operations and told residents of the devastated shoreline in Soma, the worst hit town in Fukushima prefecture, to run to safety.

They barked out orders. `Find higher ground. Get out of here!" Several soldiers were seen leading an old woman up a muddy hillside. The warning turned out to be a false alarm and interrupted the efforts of search parties who arrived in Soma for the first time since Friday to dig out bodies out of the rubble. Their job was to search and find bodies under the rubble.

Ambulances stood by and body bags were laid out in an area cleared of debris, as firefighters used hand picks and chain saws to clear a jumble of broken timber, plastic sheets, roofs, sludge, twisted cars, tangled power lines and household goods.

Ships were tipped over near roads, a half-mile (a kilometer) inland Officials said one-third of the city of 38,000 people was flooded and thousands were missing.

Though Japanese officials have refused to speculate on how the death toll could be increased, an expert who dealt with the 2004 Asian tsunami offered a dire outlook.

"It's a miracle really, if it turns out to be less than 10,000" dead, said Hery Herjono geologist with the Indonesian Science Institute, who was closely involved with the aftermath of the earlier disaster that killed 230,000 people – of which only 184,000 bodies were found.

He drew parallels between the two disasters – notably that many bodies in Japan may have been sucked out to sea or remain trapped beneath rubble as they did in Indonesia's hardest-hit Aceh province. But he also stressed that Japan's infrastructure, high-level of preparedness and city planning to keep houses away from the shore could mitigate its human losses.

According to public broadcast NHK, some 430,000 people were living in emergency shelters or with relatives. Another 24,000 people are stranded, it said. The earthquake and tsunami have put them in a world of their own and no where to turn to.

The reason for the loss of power was the damage to several nuclear reactors in the area. At one plant, Fukushima Daiichi, three reactors have lost the ability to cool down. A building holding one of them exploded on Monday. Operators were dumping sea water into all three reactors in a final attempt to cool their superheated containers that faced possible meltdown. If that happened, they could release radioactive material in the air.

Though people living within a 12 mile (20 kilometer) radius were ordered to leave over the weekend, as authorities told anyone remaining there or in nearby areas to stay inside their homes following the blast. The government was warning people in that area of the outcome.

So far, Tokyo Electric Power, the nuclear plant's operator was holding off on imposing the rolling blackouts it earlier said it would need, but the utility urged people to limit electricity use. To help the power load, and many regional train lines were suspended or operating a limited schedule.

The impact that lack of electricity damaged roads and railways and ruined plants would have on the world's third-largest economy helped drag down the share markets on Monday, the first business day since the disasters. The benchmark Nikkei 225 percent was while the broader Topic index lost 7.5 percent.

To lessen the damage, Japan's central bank injected 15 trillion (US$184 billion) into money markets.

Beyond the stock exchange, recovering from the disaster was likely to weigh on already debt-burden Japan, which has barely managed weak growth between slowdowns for over 20 years.

Initial estimates put repair costs in the tens of billions, and costs that would likely add to a massive public debt at 200 percent of gross domestic product, and was the biggest among industrialized nations.

CHAPTER EIGHT

Koriyama, Japan – Japan's nuclear crisis intensified on Sunday as authorities raced to combat the threat of multiple reactor meltdowns and more than 170,000 people evacuated from the quake and tsunami savaged northeastern coast where fears spread over possible radioactive contamination.

The Nuclear plant operators were frantically trying to keep temperatures down in series of nuclear reactors – including one where officials feared a partial meltdown could be happening on Sunday – to prevent the disaster from growing worse, several precautions would have to be taken to prevent the situation from getting any worse.

Chief Cabinet Secretary Yukio Edano also said that a hydrogen explosion could occur at Unit 3 of the Fukushima Daiichi nuclear complex and the latest reactor to face a possible meltdown. That would follow a blast the day before in the power Unit 1, and operators attempted to prevent a meltdown there by injecting sea water into it. They had the do their best to cool it down and the only water available to them was sea water. They were trying their best to cut down the radiation to the nearby people of the plant.

"At the risk of raising further public concern, they couldn't rule out the possibility of an explosion," Edano said. "If there was an explosion, however, there would be no significant impact on human health." Edano was not telling the people the truth, if there was an explosion, it would be a real impact to human health.

More that 170,000 people had been evacuated as a precaution, though

Edano said the radioactive release into the environment so far was so small, it didn't pose any health threats.

"First, I was worried about the quake," Kenji Koshiba, a construction worker who lives near the plant. "Now I'm worried about radiation." He spoke at an emergency center in Koriyama town near the power plant in Fukushima.

The French Embassy urged the citizens on Sunday to leave the area around Tokyo – 170 miles (270 kilometers) from Fukushima Daiichi in case the crisis deepened and a "radioactive plume" headed for the area around the capital. The statement acknowledged that the possibility was looking unlikely.

Edano said none of the Fukushima Daiichi reactors were near the point of a complete meltdown and he was confident of escaping the worst scenarios.

A complete meltdown – the collapse of a power plant's ability to keep temperatures under control – could release uranium and dangerous contaminants into the environment and poses major, and widespread health risks for the residents of that area.

Up to 160 people including 60 elderly patients and medical staff who had been waiting for evacuation in the nearby town of Futable, and 100 others evacuating by bus, might have been exposed to radiation, said Ryo Miyake, a spokesman from Japan nuclear agency. It was the severity of the exposure, or if it had reached such dangerous levels and that was not clear. They were being taken to hospitals.

Edano said operators were trying to cool and decrease the pressure in the 3 reactor, and just as they had the day before at Unit 1.

"We're taking measures on Unit 3 based on similar possibility of a partial meltdown," Edano said.

Japan struggled with the nuclear crisis as it tried to determine the scale of the Friday disasters, when an 8.9 magnitude earthquake, and the most powerful in the country's recorded history, was followed by a tsunami that savaged its northeastern coast with breathtaking speed and power, and crushed everything in sight.

More than 1,400 people were killed and hundreds more were missing, according to officials, but the police in one of the worst-hit areas estimated the toll there alone could eventually be over 10,000 residents.

The scale of the multiple disasters appeared to be outpacing the efforts of Japanese authorities to bring the situation under control more than two days after the initial quake.

Rescue teams were struggling to search hundreds of miles (kilometers) of devastated coastline and hundreds of thousands of hungry survivors huddled in darkened emergency centers cut off from rescuers and aid. At least 1 4 million thousands had gone without water since the quake and food and gasoline were quickly running out across the region. Large areas of the countryside were surrounded by water and unreachable. Some 2 million households were without electricity.

Japanese Trade Minister Bann Kaieda warned that the region was likely to face further blackouts and would be rationed to ensure supplies to essential facilities.

The government doubled the number of troops pressed into the recovery operations to about 100,000 from 51,000, as powerful aftershocks to rock the country. Hundreds have since experienced the initial temblor.

Unit 3 at the Fukushima plant is one of three reactors there that had automatically shut down and lost cooling functions necessary to keep fuel rods working properly due to a power outage from the quake. The facility's Unit 1 was also in trouble, but Unit 2 has been less affected.

On Saturday, an explosion destroyed the walls of Unit 1 as operators desperately tried to prevent it from overheating and melting down.

Without power, and with its valves and pumps damaged by the tsunami, authorities resorted to drawing sea water mixed with boron in an attempt to cool the unit's overheated uranium rods. Boron disrupts nuclear chain reactions.

To move likely tenders the 40-year-old reactor unusable, said a foreign ministry official briefing reporters. Officials said the sea water will remain inside the unit, possibly for several months.

Robert Alvarez, senior scholar at the Institute for Policy Studies and former senior policy adviser to the US secretary of energy, told reporters that the sea water was a desperate measure.

He said that the success of using sea water and boron to cool the reactor will depend on the volume and rate of their distribution. He said the dousing would need to continue nonstop for days.

Another key, he said was the restoration of electrical power, so that normal cooling systems can operate.

Edano said the cooling operation at Unit 1 was going smoothly after the sea water was pumped in.

Operators released slightly radioactive air from Unit 3 on Sunday, while injecting water into it hoping to reduce pressure and temperature to prevent a possible meltdown, Edano said.

He said radiation level just outside the plant briefly rose above legal limits, but since it had declined significantly. Also, fuel rods were exposed briefly, he said, indicating that coolant water didn't cover rods for some time. That would have contributed further to raising the temperature in the reactor vessel.

At an evacuation center in Konyama about 40 miles (60 kilometers) from the troubled reactors and 125 miles (190 kilometers) north of Tokyo, medical experts had experts had checked about 1,500 people for radiation exposure in an emergency testing center, an official said.

On Sunday, a few people waited to be checked in a collection of blue tents set up in a parking lot outside a local gymnasium. Fire engines surrounded the scene, with their lights flashing.

Many of the gym's windows were shattered by the quake, and glass shards littered the ground.

A steady flow of people – the elderly, schoolchildren and families with babies arrived at the center, where they were checked by officials wearing helmets, surgical masks and goggles.

Officials placed five reactors, including Units 1 and 3 at Daiichi, under states of emergency Friday after operators lost ability to cooling the reactors using usual procedures.

An additional reactor was added to the list early on Sunday, for a total of six – three at the Daiichi complex and three at another nearby complex. Local evacuations have been ordered at each location. Japan has a total 55 reactors, which are spread across 17 complexes nationwide.

Officials began venting radioactive steam at Fukushima Daiichi's Unit 1 to relieve pressure inside the reactor vessel, which houses the overhead uranium fuel.

Concerns escalated on Saturday when that unit's containment exploded.

Officials were aware that the steam contained hydrogen and were risking an explosion by venting it, and acknowledged Shinji Sinjo, spokesman for the government Nuclear and Industrial Safety Agency, but chose to do so because they needed to keep circulating cool water on the fuel rods to prevent a meltdown.

Officials insisted there was no significant radioactive leak after the explosion.

If a full scale meltdown were to occur, experts interviewed by The Associated Press said, melted fuel would eat through the bottom of the reactor vessel, then through the floor of the containment building. At that point, the uranium and dangerous byproducts would start escaping into the environment.

Eventually the walls of the reactor vessel – six inches (15 centimeters) of stainless steel – would melt into a lava-like pile, sump into any remaining water on the floor, and potentially cause an explosion that would entrance the spread of radioactive containments.

If the reactor core became expose to the outside, officials would likely began pouring cement and sand over the entire facility, as was done at the 1986 Chemobyl nuclear accident in the Ukraine, Peter Bradford, a former commissioner of the U.S. Nuclear Regulatory Commission, told reporters.

Another expert physicist Ken Bergeron, told reporters that as a result of such a meltdown, the surrounding land would be off-limits for residents for a long time and "a lot of first responders would die.

CHAPTER NINE

Water, power and food were scarce in the vast swaths of Japan:

Tagajo, Japan – People across a devastated swath of Japan suffered a third day on Sunday without water, electricity and proper food, as the country grappled with the enormity of a massive earthquake and tsunami that left more than 10,000 people dead in one area alone. It was a prime story of those who were left dead, and the government would have to take care of that whole bad situation.

Japan's Prime Minister, Kan called the crisis the most severe challenge the nation has had to face since World War II, as the grim situation worsened on Friday's disasters damaged a series of nuclear reactors, potentially sending one through a partial meltdown and adding radiation contamination to the fears of an unsettled public. This was very bad news for the citizens of the area, who were still alive.

Temperatures began sinking toward a freezing point, compounding the misery of survivors along hundreds of miles (kilometers) of northeastern coast which was battered by the tsunami that smashed inland with breathtaking fury. Rescuers pulled bodies from mud-covered jumbles of wrecked houses, shattered tree trunks, twisted cars and tangled power lines while survivors examined the ruined remains.

In Rikusentakata, a port city of over 20,000 virtually wiped out by the tsunami. Etsuko Koyama escaped the water rushing through the third floor of her home, but lost her grip on her daughter's hand and has not found her. Her daughter was swept away by the large wave of the tsunami, and there was nothing she could do but to cry out in despair.

"I haven't given up hope yet," Koyama told public broadcaster NHK, wiping tears from her eyes. "I saved myself, but I couldn't save my daughter."

To the south, in Miyagi prefecture, or state, the police chief told a gathering of disaster relief officials that his estimated for deaths were more than 10,000, a police spokesman Go Sugawara told The Associated Press.

Miyagi has a population of 2.3 million and is one of the three prefectures hardest hit on Friday's disaster. Fewer that 400 people have officially been confirmed as dead in Miyagi.

According to officials, more than 1,400 people were killed – including 200 people whose bodies were found on Sunday along the coast and more than 1,000 were missing in the disasters. Another 1,700 residents were injured.

Japanese officials raised their estimate on Sunday of the quake magnitude to 9.0 of a notch above the U.S. Geological Survey's reading of 8.9. Either way, it was the strongest quake ever recorded in Japan.

In Japan one of the workers' leading economies with ultramodern infrastructure, and at that time the disasters plunged ordinary life into nearly unimaginable deprivation.

Hundreds of thousands of hungry survivors huddled in darkened emergency centers that were cut off from rescuers, and from aid and electricity. At last 1.4 million households had gone without water since the quake struck on Friday, and some 1.9 million households were without electricity.

While the government doubled the number of soldiers deployed in the aid effort to 100,000 and sent 120,000 blankets, 120,000 bottles of water and 29,000 gallons (110,000 liters) of gasoline plus food to the affected areas. Prime Minister Naoto Kan said electricity would take days to restore. In the meantime, he said electricity would be rationed with rolling blackouts to several areas, including Tokyo.

"This is Japan's most severe crisis since the war ended 65 years ago," Kan told reporters, adding that Japan's future would be decided by its response.

In a rare piece of good news, the Defense Ministry said a military vessel on Sunday rescued a 60-year-old man, Emiko, was floating off the coast of Fukushima on the roof of his house after he and his wife were swept away in the tsunami. He was in good condition. His wife did not survive. She was swept away into the sea and the sea had taken her life away. He was alive and devastated by the lost of his beloved wife, Asano.

A young man described what ran through his mind before he escaped in a separate rescue. "I thought to myself, ah, this is how I will die," Tatsuro Ishikawa, his face bruised and cut, he told NHK as he sat in striped hospital pajamas.

Dozens of countries have offered assistance. Two US aircraft carrier groups were off Japan's coast and ready to provide assistance. Helicopters were flying from one of the carriers, the USS Ronald Reagan delivering food and water in Miyagi.

Two other U.S. rescue teams of 72 personnel each and rescue dogs arrived on Sunday, as did a five-dog team from Singapore. They were willing to help in whatever way possible.

Still larger areas of the countryside remained surrounded by water and unreachable for assistance. Fuel stations were closed, though, at some, cars waited in lines of hundreds of vehicles in line, and everyone took their turn in a respective way.

The United States and several countries in Europe urged their citizens to avoid travel to Japan. France took the added step of suggesting people leave Tokyo in case radiation reached the city.

Community after community traced the vast extent of the devastation. In the town of Minamisanrkucho, 10,000 people – nearly two-thirds of the population have not been heard from since the tsunami wiped it out, a government spokesman said NHK showed only a couple concrete structures still standing and the bottom three floors of those buildings gutted. One of the few buildings still standing was a hospital and a worker told NHK that the hospital staff rescued about a third of the patients in the facility. In the town of Iwaki, there was no electricity, stores were closed and residents left as food and fuel supplies dwindled. Local police took in about 90 people and they gave them blankets and rice balls, but there was no sign of government or military aid trucks in that area.

At a large refinery on the outskirts of the hard-hit port city of Sendai, 100 foot (30 meter) – high bright orange flames rose in the air, and spitting out dark plumes of smoke. The facility has been burning since Friday. The fire's roar could be heard from far away. Smoke burned the eyes and throat of residents in that area, and a gaseous stench was hug in the air.

The small town of Tagajo, also near Sendai dazed residents roamed the streets, which was cluttered with smashed cars, broken homes and twisted metal. The whole area was in a mess by the earthquake and tsunami.

Residents said the water surged in and quickly rose higher than the first floor of buildings. At Sengen General Hospital, the staff worked feverishly to haul bedridden patients up the stars, one at a time. With the halls now dark and those who could leave have gone to the local community centers.

"There is still no water or power, and we've some very sick people here," said hospital official Ikuro Matsumoto.

Police cars drove slowly through the town and warned residents through loudspeakers to seek higher ground, but most simply stood by and watch them pass.

In Sendai, firefighters with wooden picks dug through a devastated area neighborhood. One of them yelled "A corpse". Inside a house, he had found the body of a gray-haired woman under a blanket.

A few minutes later, the firefighter spotted another – that of a man in black fleece jacket and pants, crumpled in a partial fetal position at the bottom of a wooden stairwell. From outside, while the top of the house seemed almost untouched, the first floor where the body was had been inundated. A minivan lay embedded in one outlet wall, which had been ripped away, pulverized beside a mangled bicycle.

The main neighbor, 24-year-old Ayumi Osuga, dug through the remains of her own house, and she did this with her white mittens that were covered by dark mud.

Osuga said she had been practicing origami, in Japanese at of folding paper into figures, with her three children when the quake struck. She recalled her husband's shouted warning from outside. "Get out of there now." She knew immediately what was going to happen next. The tsunami was on its way and many would die in a watery grave.

She gathered the children – aged 2 to 6 – and fled in her car to higher ground with her husband. They spent the night in a hilltop home belonging to her husband's family about 12 miles (20 kilometers) away. Osuga was very smart and she knew what was going to happen and she made her way up the hill with her beloved family, and all was well and not lost. "My family and my children are lucky to be alive," Osuga said and she was grateful for the opportunity to be alive.

"I have come to realize what is important in life," Osuga said, nervously flicking ashes from a cigarette onto the rubble at her feet as a giant column of black smoke billowed in the distance. But little did she know that she had left a lot of misery behind, and she was grateful that she and her family were still alive, while the other resident below had met with a dim fate.

CHAPTER TEN

It was Sunday and it was surprising how those wonderful people of Japan were facing life after the earthquake and tsunami. They are a strong and proud people, and they really knew what suffering was all about. After the earthquake and tsunami, they had to bury their dead, and they had to do their mourning for any of the family who did not make it. But after their cries and tears, they would start rebuilding their towns and their villages. Their great island would be the place to make them strong again and also to give them life, and replacing all those who were washed away by the tsunami. Their lives were in vain.

They now knew what they had to do and if they were alive, they would have to go to the rescue center, and there they would meet other people to comfort them. Some food and water would be there for them, but they were well trained and with only a small ball of rice and some water to quench their hunger. Their dreams were still outside and no earthquake and tsunami would take their proud attitude away. They felt once everything was settled, they would start to rebuild their homes, which were near to the shores – they considered that the shores were too near to the sea, and they considered that the sea was part of their lives, but in theory they should be moving away from near to the shores and away from the sea, because the sea had taken so many of their lives, but their lives depended upon the sea, even though the sea had taken over 10,000 lives this time and many other lives before, in the towns, Tagajo, Koriyama and Miayagi, which were considered the worst eras of the northeast of Japan.

It could never believe the tsunami had washed away several thousands people into the sea, and the sea was now their graves. They never had a chance and those left behind would be forced to bury those who were found ashore and in rubble, but in theory they were buried. They got rid of the bodies by cremation. Each time anything like that happens, that's how they got rid of the bodies and the living had to do that. They were a strong and proud people and they did their own thing, and they didn't ask any questions and they didn't ask for any help from other countries. They felt it was their dead and they had to bury the people who were unfortunate in the disaster of time.

They had the world looking at them and loving them for their proud attitude.

They were going to remove all the debris from all over the land, so their lives could continue again – the rest of their belongings went out to sea – floating away from Japan – their dreams – their lives were floating away. It was left for them to rebuild and continue with their real lives on shore.

They knew the whole world would be watching to see what they would do, and at that turn they would be more determined to do the just thing and rebuild their towns and villages, and find out where they went wrong, but that will be something they would never know for sure.

CHAPTER ELEVEN

Japan confronted devastations along its northeastern coast on Saturday, with fires raging and parts of some cities under water after a massive earthquake and tsunami that likely killed at least 1,000 people in that area.

Daybreak was expected to reveal the full extent of the deaths and damages from Friday's 8.9 magnitude earthquake and the 10-meter high tsunami it sent surging into cities and villages, sweeping away everything in its path. The people of Japan were not expecting such a massive earthquake and in just several minutes several thousands of people were killed. They certainly didn't expect to die that way by a tsunami, but the natural way one dies.

In one of the worst hit residential areas, people buried under rubble and they could be heard calling for "help" and when are we going to be rescued," Kyodo news agency reported.

The government warned there could be a small radiation leak from a nuclear reactor whose cooling system was knocked out by the quake. Prime Minister Naoto Kan ordered an evacuation zone around the plant be expanded to 10 km (6 miles) from 3km. Some 3,000 people had earlier been moved out of harm's way.

Underscoring concerns about the Fukushima plant, 240 km (150 miles) north of Tokyo, US officials said Japan had asked for coolant to avert a rise in the temperature of its nuclear rods, but ultimately handled the matter on its own. Officials said a leak was still possible because pressure would have to be released.

The unfolding natural disaster prompted offers of search and rescue help from 45 countries.

China said rescuers were ready to help with quake relief while President Barack Obama told Japanese Prime Minister Naoto Kan the United States would assist in any way possible. The Prime Minister didn't want any help from the U.S. but he had no choice, he had to accept any help from other countries. He was learning to take as you get, and be friendly with other countries.

"This is likely to be a humanitarian relief operation of epic proportions," Japan expert Sheila Smith of the US – based Council on Foreign Relations wrote in a commentary. At that time all eyes were on Japan.

The northeastern Japanese city of Kesennuma, with a population of 74,000, was hit by widespread fires and one-third of the city was under water, Jiji news agency said on Saturday.

The airport in the city of Sendai, home to one million people, was on fire, it added. This was very bad news to the residents in that area.

TV footage from Friday showed a muddy torrent of water carrying cars and wrecked homes at a high speed across farmland near Sedai, 300 km (180 miles) northeast of Tokyo. Ships had been flung into the harbor wharf, where they lay helplessly on their side.

Boats, cars and trucks were tossed around like toys in the water after a small tsunami hit the town of Kamaichi in northern Japan. Kyodo news agency reported that contact had been lost with four trains in the coastal area.

Japanese politicians pushed for an emergency budget to fund relief efforts after Kan asked them to' save the country,' Kyodo news agency reported. Japan is already the most heavily indebted major economy in the world, meaning any funding efforts would be closely scrutinized.

Domestic media said the death toll was expected to exceed 1,000, most of who appeared to have drowned by churning waters.

The extent of the destruction along a lengthy stretch of coastline suggests the death toll could rise significantly

Even in a nation accustomed to earthquakes, the devastation was shocking.

"A big area of Sendai city near the coast was flooded. We are hearing that people who were evacuated are stranded," said Rie Sugimota, a reporter for NHK television in Sendai.

"About 140 people, including children, were rushed to an elementary school and were on the rooftop, but they were surrounded by water and have nowhere else to go."

Japan has pride itself on its speedy tsunami system, which has been upgraded several times since its inspection in 1952, including after a 7.8 magnitude quake triggered a 30-meter high wave before a warning was given. Its warning had to be precise, so as to save lives, so that people had to run for their lives to higher ground.

The country has also built countless breakwaters and floodgates to protect ports and coastal areas, although experts said they might not have been enough to prevent disasters such as the one that truck on Friday.

In Tokyo many residents who had earlier fled swaying buildings slept in their offices after public was shut down. Many subways in Tokyo later resumed operation but trains did not run.

"I was unable to stay on my feet because of the violent shaking. The aftershocks gave us no reprieve. Then the tsunami came when we tried to run for cover. It was the strongest quake I experienced," a woman with a baby on her back told television in northern Japan.

Fires across the coast:

The quake, the most powerful since Japan started keeping records 140 years ago, sparked at least 80 fires in cities and towns along the coast, Kyado said.

Other Japanese nuclear power plants and oil refineries were shut down and one refinery was ablaze.

Auto plants, electronics factories and refineries shut, roads buckled and power to millions of homes and businesses was knocked out. Several airports, including Tokyo's Narita, were closed and rail services halted. All ports were shut.

The central bank said it would cut short a two day policy review scheduled for next week to one day on Monday and promised to do its utmost to ensure financial market stability.

The disaster occurred at the world's third-largest economy had been showing signs of reviving from an economic contraction in the final quarter of last year. It raised the prospect of major disruptions for many key businesses and a massive repair bill running into tens of billions of dollars.

The tsunami alerts revived memories of the giant waves that struck Asia in 2004.

Warnings were issued for countries to the west of Japan and across the

Pacific as far away as Colombia and Peru, but the tsunami dissipated as it sped across the ocean and worst fears in the Americas were not realized.

The earthquake was the fifth most powerful to hit the world in the past century.

The building shook for what seemed a long time and many people in the newsroom grabbed their helmets and some got under their desks," Reuters correspondent Linda Sieg said in Tokyo. "It was probably the worst I have felt since I came to Japan more than 20 years ago."

The quake surpasses the Great Kanto quake of September 1, 1923, which had a magnitude of 7.9 and killed more than 140,000 people in the Tokyo area.

The 1995 Kobe quake caused $100 billion in damage and was the most expensive natural disaster in history. Economic damage from the 2004 Indian Ocean tsunami was estimated at about $10 billion.

Earthquakes are common in Japan, one of the world's most seismically active areas. The whole island faces all the bad aspects of disaster, volcanoes, earthquakes, tsunamis and other disasters of other kinds, and the residents of Japan are accustomed to such disasters. Bless them all!

CHAPTER TWELVE

Amid Japan's Earthquake Ruin, a Father Seeks His Daughter:
Bowlegged and rheumy-eyed, 76-year-old farmer Masahira Kasamatsu barreled down the sodden path. His pants were rolled above his knees and his shoeless feet were covered with inky mud deposited by the tsunami that had swept across northeastern Japan three days earlier, killing thousands upon thousands of people. I'm looking for my daughter," he said, barely breaking his stride as he negotiated fallen electricity poles and mangled cars. Her name is Yoko Oosato. Have you seen her?" he asked nervously.

Kasamatsu's daughter had worked for 30 years at the airport in Sendai, the largest city in the devastated region. After 8.9 magnitude earthquake, the worst in Japan's history, struck on March 11, the costal airport was deluged by a 10m-high wave of water that churned up debris and mud several kilometers inland. Hundreds of upturned cars, airplanes and trucks littered the waterlogged landscape.

For three days, Kasamatus, whose home had been flooded by the tsunami, called his daughter's cell phone to no avail. He listened to the death rolls on the radio. He did not hear her name. Finally, Kasamatsu and his wife, Emiko, climbed into their car and drove toward the airport. The roads were barely passable, petrol ran out. The couple spent the night in their unheated car before he abandoned the vehicle and began desperately wading through water and mud to get to the airport. At this stage he was desperate to find his beloved daughter, Oosato.

"I know there are so many people that are dead," he said, as we entered the terminal building, passing 6-m-high piles of cars and uprooted planes.

A pair of discarded sandals sat nearly in front of the domestic terminal. "I know that my daughter may be just one more person among so many dead. But my deepest hope is that she is still alive. That is my only prayer at this moment."

Across northern Japan invocations were being uttered by family members who still had no idea whether their loved ones were alive or dead. Tens of thousands of people were still unaccounted for, and radio stations laboriously relayed information about centenarians looking for their relatives or dead children identified by their birthmarks. Cell-phone networks were down in much of the region, and vast lakes formed by the tsunami rendered roads impassable.

With food, water and gas running low, lines of people snaked through towns in stretches of several kilometers, waiting patiently for whatever sustenance could be found, even as temperatures dipped toward freezing. Adding to the distress, nuclear reactors in Fukushima prefecture were in danger of suffering meltdowns as a result of the quake and tsunami, sending radioactive material into the air which was already bustling with tragedy. On Sunday, Japan Prime Minister Naoto Kan called the triple whammy of earthquake, tsunami and possible nuclear fallout of the country's 'worst crisis' since World War II.

In Miyagi, a group of students from the Civil Aviation College floated in an inflatable yellow raft across what was dry land just three days ago. Some 170 students and airplane maintenance employees had watched the tsunami roll in from the roof of a school building where they had decamped after the earthquake triggered a tsunami alert that was broadcast on loudspeakers, radios and TVs. "The tsunami came toward us so slowly that it was hard to understand what was approaching," recalled Satoshi Tsuchira, a 24. "But then it came and kept on coming and I wondered if it would ever end."

A 10-m-high wave of water marooned their building and sent a churning mass of vehicles, planes and houses swirling past them. The students kept their eyes on a solitary man who clung to the top of a bobbing truck for a night and gasped as the receding waters pulled dozens of cars out to sea. Those stranded on the roof had only one box of energy cookies for every four individuals. Rationing began, and a cold rain continued. On a near by road, a forlorn piano lay on its side, along with an office stripped of its wall. After more than 24 hours, the fire department arrived to rescue the strapped students. As they ferried some of their belongings from their dorm to higher ground, the prospect of a radioactive cloud possible making its way toward them was too much to comprehend. "We have suffered through an earthquake and a tsunami," said Koutaro Nousou. "Our college is underwater. I can't deal with another disaster. It's just too much."

The students gathered up their things to an unheated evacuation center, where they would sleep on one or two blankets. Masahira Kasamatsu was making his way to the Sendai airport. Entering the terminal, he climbed up a suspended escalator that wobbled under his weight and quietly approached a man in gray jacket who looked like he was in charge. His name was Kenichi Numata. After suffering through the earthquake, Numata immediately headed to the designated high ground – in his case the airport – as he had been taught in the tsunami drills conducted up and down coastal Japan. Numate had watched from the airport as dozens of people succumbed in the surrounding water. He now knew that his house had washed away. "Everything is gone," he said with a sweep of his hand. "It's all gone."

But there was time to process this loss. Numata had been designated as one of the section leaders organizing the 1,600 people initially stranded at the Sendai airport. They had been completely cut off, with no cell-phone access or information about what had be befallen the rest of the region. "What is your daughter's name, again?" he asked Kasamatsu . The farmer slowly repeated her name and stared into the middle distance. Numata and others conferred. "Yoko Oosato, is it," Numata said. "Why, she went home just a little while ago. "It took a moment for Kasamatsu to process the news. He nodded slowly. "She's OK," he repeated, as if to convince himself. "She's OK."

We drove Kasamatsu through the floodwaters back to his wife, who was waiting beside their car, mangled vehicles and twisted buildings all around. As we approached, she drove into her car to offer me an armful of oranges and apples in gratitude for having her husband back from the airport. Only as she gathered up the fruit did their eyes meet. "And Yoko?" she asked her husband. "She's OK," Kasamatsu replied. "She's OK," There were no hugs or overwhelming expressions of elation. Their daughter had been spared. But devastation was still around.

This was a very dramatic story of a father's love for his daughter and he and his wife went to the Sendai's airport to find her. "Only to be told that Yoko Oosato's daughter was alive and she just went home."

CHAPTER THIRTEEN

Survivors waiting for assistance:

Minami Soma, Japan. The farm house sit at the end of a mud-caked, one-lane road strewn with toppled trees, the decaying carcasses of dead pigs and a large debris deposited by the March 11, tsunami.

Stranded alone inside the unheated dark home was 75-year-old Kunio Shiga. He cannot walk very far and doesn't know what happened to his wife. She just disappeared from him after the tsunami and she hadn't come back, and he was left all alone, hungry and helpless. He cried out for help, but no one was around to hear him. He was left all alone.

His neighbors have left because they had no choice, but to run for their lives, when the tsunami came their way. They left the area because the area is 20 kilometers from the crippled Fukushima Dai-ichi nuclear plant – which was just within the zone where authorities have told everyone to get out because of concerns about leaking radiation. This was really bad news for the residents of that area.

No rescuer ever came for Shiga. He was left all alone to die in his own house.

When a reporter and two photographers from The Associated Press arrived at Shiga's doorsteps on Friday, the scared and disoriented farmer said: "You are the first people I have seen and spoken to since the earthquake and tsunami. Do you have any food?" he asked because he was hungry. "I will pay you," Shiga gratefully accepted the one-liter bottle of water and a sack of 15-20 energy bars given to him by the AP, which later notified local police of his situation. They really wanted Shiga to have some help from the authorities.

He said he has been running out of supplies and he was unable to cook his rice for lack of electricity and running water. Traditionally, his two storey house was intact, although it was a mess of fallen objects, including a toppled Buddhist shrine. Temperatures at night in the region have been cold, but it was above freezing.

The Odaka neighborhood where he lives was a ghost town. Neighboring fields were still inundated from the tsunami. The smell of the sea was everywhere. The only noise comes from the pigs foraging for food.

"The tsunami came right up to my doorsteps," he said. "I don't know what happened to my wife. She was here, but now she's gone."

Even if the authorities can make it to him, Shiga said he might rather stay.

"I'm old and I don't know if I could leave here. Who would take care of me?" he said, staring blankly through his sliding glass doors at the mess in his yard. "I don't want to go anywhere. I don't have water and I'm running out of food."

It was not know if Shiga wife was washed away by the tsunami, because after days she was not to be found. He was left all alone to die in his own house and he wasn't going to go with the authorities. Bless him for all that he is worth.

Kunio Shiga, after the reporters left, he started to listen to a battery-powered radio in the living room of his home in Minami Soma, Fukushima Prefecture.

These are some of the dramatic stories you would hear throughout that area of Fukushima.

CHAPTER FOURTEEN

Tokyo – For days on end, 23-year-old Hiraku Sato and a co-worker toiled in their pharmacy in Tagajo City, picking through hundreds of small containers of vitamin drinks, aspirin and other medicines that were flung to the four corners of their shop when ocean waters from a kilometer away rushed in their store.

A meter high mound of metal shelves, broken computers and other retail detritus was still massed last week outside the store in the northeastern coastal community. But Sato, wearing a white mask and knee-high rubber boots, and he was beamed with satisfaction at what he had organized inside: blue, green and pink baskets packed with unopened but mud-caked bottles and boxes.

"I was really upset when I came here and saw the mess," he said. But now that he's been able to salvage a few things, he added, he could see hope for recovery – never mind that customers might not want the dirty products, or that the street outside still looked like a total wasteland.

"I don't know when, where or how they'll clean this up," he sighed.

In the best of times, one man's trash is another man's treasure. But it was in the wake of Japan's March 11 earthquake and tsunami, that the nation was now facing a complex, legal, financial, logistical, environmental, and ethical questions over just how to deal with at least 73 million tones of debris – from 300-tone ships and smashed cars to waterlogged heirlooms and soiled family photos. The whole situation was in a mess and it would need a lot of labor to clean up the mess. This would be the worse part when the tsunami struck on land, and leaving a mess behind.

The central government says it would foot the bill for the clean up, and normally, it covers half of the local governments' waste-disposal cost. The expense was beginning to be tabulated, but it's expected to far exceed the $3.2 billion required to dispose of 14 million tones of debris in Kobe after it 1995 earthquake.

Still being sorted out were such nitty-gritty questions as: How long will owners pg waterlogged autos – who might need their license plates to file insurance claims – be given to claim their vehicles? Can cleanup crews unilaterally bulldoze structures, or do they need approval from property owners? What should be done if sentimental or valuable items were recovered amid the junk?

Certain valuables already pose their own challenges for Japan Self-Defense Forces troops working in southern Miyagi prefecture reportedly came across a 20-kilogram safe beneath a collapsed house. They couldn't open it, and there was nothing to indicate where it came from.

Waste management specialists were now debating whether the vast amount of debris – called gareki in Japanese – can be tested for toxins such as asbestos can't disperse into the air. But when the dry season arrives, dangerous particles could be inhaled. And then, of course, there were fears of radiation contamination from the quake-crippled Fukushima nuclear plant.

For the time being, parks, baseball fields and stadiums were being used as temporary dumps. But longer term, there would be serious questions about where in an already space-challenged island nation the trash can be disposed of.

Japan's National Police Agency says 18,000 houses collapsed and that about 140,000 others were partially damaged. In Miyagi prefecture alone, an estimated 146,000 cars were destroyed and more may yet be found as tsunami-inundated areas dry out.

The trash problems extend beyond the quake and tsunami zone. In Tokyo, which normally burns trash 24 hours a day, everyday garbage was piling up because post-quake power shortages have forced incinerators to curtail operations by as much as a third.

Additional refuse washed out to sea and was expected to reach Hawaii in about two years and Alaska a year later, according to Nikolal Maximenko, an oceanographer at the University of Hawaii who studies ocean currents.

In normal times, Japan's meticulous approach to waste and recycling the stuff of legend, and it was not just a matter of separating paper from plastic, or glass from aluminum – cities here publish detailed guides for properly disposing of everything from used chopsticks to lipstick.

Special bags must be used. Collection schedules are strict. To ignore the rules is a risk being reprimanded by a local volunteer trash monitor, or shunned by neighbors

But there was no rule book for problems such as the 500,000 tones of rotting seafood in disabled port refrigeration facilities, said Massato Yamada of the National Institute for Environmental Studies, who was leading a national task force on trash crisis.

His panel has advised collecting the decaying seafood and dumping it at sea.

Recycling was further hindered because of the mud. It's not just that things are dirty, and the slop may contain toxic amounts of heavy metals from refineries, factories and other facilities smashed by the raging water.

Designating new landfills may take years, Yamada said.

For now, he and his colleagues were simply rapidly making, and the heaps can ferment and catch fire.

Waste collection has been slowed by the loss of garbage-collecting equipment and destruction of government infrastructure.

Shinji Suda, 28, a trash-collection worker in Tagajo who camped out on the upper floor of a shopping centre for two days after the tsunami, said his company's 15 garbage trucks were picked up by the wave. Only one, he said last week, had been found.

Nearly, at the New Japan Compressor Co., Hiroko Yamamoto was crying as she supervised the operation of a crane lifting stray vehicles. Normally, the crane was used to haul the heavy machines the company makes.

"We've been out of rebuilding since the second or third day," she said. "It's in our DNA."

The central government has started to impose some order on the process. Normal fees for scrapping household appliances such as air conditioners have been suspended until at least August. And the Justice Ministry if considering endorsing emergency regulations that would allow authorities to clear debris without first making contact with property owners.

Some property owners may sue the government, accusing it of getting rid of something that was still useful, but, oh well. The recovery effort has to come first, said an unnamed official on a government advisory committee quoted in the Mainichi newspaper this week.

Still, there was a keen sense that, with so many people having lost almost everything, a substantial effort must be made to reunite owners with certain keepsakes. .Volunteers were picking through muddy flats, salvaging snapshots, diplomas and other personal effects that might lift the spirits of survivors.

The government has said it will establish warehouses for things such as photo albums and ihai stones; small mortuary tables that commemorate deceased relatives and were placed on the Buddhist altar present in most Japanese homes.

CHAPTER FIFTEEN

About the nuclear power plant – too much detail – such unhappiness:

    First, the ground shook, and then the sea swallowed the land. Fires raged, lights went out, and invisible menaces seeped into the air, the water, the soil. Tears flowed and headlines were blaring tales of tragedy, sorrow and fear. All the words in the world, perhaps, could not capture the enormity of it all. The whole situation was too big for words to state what had happened to the people of Japan. No one would ever understand their plight and their sorrow that the Japanese people were facing.
    Amid the cacophony of news bulletins and tweets and cell phone alerts registering yet another aftershock, Yoshikatsu Kurota quietly sent out his brief verse. It was published, in small type, on page 14 for the mass-circulation Asahi daily, in the corner that Japan's newspapers still devote to such poetic endeavors.
    Tossed like a pebble into a lake, it made not a splash but a gentle ripple. Seventeen syllables were, radiating out into the universe, perhaps touching a few other distressed souls adrift in the chaos.
    Mere trifle to some, a quintessence of Japan to others, maligned and beloved, the haiku endures.
    In these heartsick times, aficionados of the form both here and abroad have been stirred to put brush to scroll, pen to postcard, fingers to keyboard, meshing the ancient and the modern, the sublime and the horrific.
    It is safe, but they say over and over that's worrisome:

Tadashi Nishimura's lament which, like most here, was written in Japanese and has been translated from the original 17 syllables – appeared alongside Kurota's in the pages of the Asahi. The poem distills his anxiety about officials' frequent reassurances that was fine – even as they warn day in and day out about vegetables, milk and water contaminated by radiation from the stricken nuclear power plant in Fukushima prefecture.

The two men's compositions were technically senryuu, which follows the same syllabic rules as haiku but were typically more social commentary than, say musings on natural phenomena such as the ephemeral beauty of a cherry blossom. In a culture that can seem unacquainted with sarcasm, senryuu can range for a Japanese bank whose ATM network was hobbled for days after the quake, making it difficult for victims to get much-needed cash.

Through the march of modernity has perhaps shrunk the number of regular haikuists in Japan and it has also expanded their options for airing the verses – besides the newspaper, there was a magnitude of haiku blogs, and Twitter has become a popular forum for the pint-size poems. Still there was a loyal following for haiku magazines such as Hototogisu, which dates to the late 1800s and whose title means "cuckoo."

Yasuharu You, 78, a Buddhist monk from the Shin sect who leads Kyoto's Higashi Hongan Temple, has been composing haiku since he was in school.

When a large earthquake rocked his native Niigata in October 2004, he divided under a futon as furniture and light fixtures crashed down around him. Driven out into the frigid night, unease, the haiku came to him.

The poem spread, and residents' response to it was so powerful that the haiku was eventually carved onto a memorial stone in the city.

In the wake of this month's tragedy, you composed something of a follow-up to his 2004 sensation, which Hototogistu accepted for its latest issue.

Haiku has among its devotees not only men of letters but men of science, some of them experts in the fields that have wreaked such havoc on Japan in recent days. The head of the Tokyo-based Haiku International Association, Akito Arima, is a nuclear physicist who served as president of Tokyo University, the nation's most prestigious institute of higher education. Former Kyoto University President Kazuo Oike, a seismologist, is another practitioner.

"I'm a scientist by vocation, and so looking at nature with this eye can bring new meaning" to poetry, Oike wrote in an email. Through he said he planned to bide his time before composing a new haiku, in the past two decades he often has been inspired by nature's fury, and at this time he hoped to make his mark again, and educate the residents of Japan of his theory.

CHAPTER SIXTEEN

Disaster survivors recall moments of terror:

Tagajo, Japan – Masashi Imai wrapped his arms around the wheelchair that held his disabled wife and clung on with all his strength.

Their home lurched and swayed as the ground fell away. The power went out. Imai switched on his wire radio and heard the warning. Then came the deluge.

Imai picked up his wife's limp body and cradled it and carried her to the second floor. "Father! Father!" screamed a girl from a neighboring house. Imai's wife, who has mental problems after two strokes, began to laugh. She began to laugh because she was not her true self, and everything around her was just a theory.

Many of Imai's neighbors had nowhere to run, because their houses had only one story. Eventually, the girl's voice went silent in the most powerful earthquake ever recorded in Japan, the line between life and death proved very thin – just one story high, in Imai's case, or little more than a bus length away from a wall of water. Even along the killing zone of the northeastern coast, some buildings and entire neighborhoods were spared while others were obliterated. The death toll was feared to be higher than 10,000.

On that fateful Friday, Ayumi Osuga was practicing origami with her three children, aged 2 to 6, in their single-story home in the costal city of Sendai. At 2:46 p.m., the ground started to shake. Cups and plates fell from cupboards and shattered, but the damage seemed minor.

Then Osuga's husband called, "Get out of there now!" he yelled.

Chilled by the brusque warning, the 24-old factory worker quickly gathered her children into the car and fled to a hilltop home belonging to her husband's family 12 miles (20 kilometers) away. She managed to beat the large waves that were moving behind her at the speed of a jumbo jet. She was so scared that she didn't look back behind her.

She was safe on the higher ground and Osuga's family spent the night listening to the radio. The darkness was lit only by candles, and the cold was bitter and some snow still lay on the hills around. But the main aspect was that the Osuga's family was safe, while others were not that safe.

On Sunday, she returned with her husband and relatives to a home that was no more. Among the only things that had survived were three large packs of diapers. Tears were in her eyes. Osuga stuffed the diapers, along with ruin bank documents and family photos into backpacks.

Osuga was hoping the neighborhood had been spared of any deaths. But just then, a team of firefighters with wooden picks appeared. One of them yelled out "a corpse". "Inside a house about 15 yards (meters) away, and they found the body of a gray-haired woman lying under a blanket.

A few minutes later, the firefighters spotted another. It was Osuga's neighbor. Wearing a black fleece and black pants and he lay crumpled in a partial fetal position, hugging some cardboard debris and at the bottom of a muddy wooden stairwell inside his home.

Then the walkway started swaying badly, and they ran down into the street. People

The top of the house appeared almost mockingly untouched – with just two cracks in the white wall, and a small satellite dish was still dotting the blue tiled roof.

Osuga knew she was lucky to be alive. "My family and my children, I have come to realize what is important in life," she said proudly. She realized that immediately because some of her neighbors were dead and she and her family was alive.

As Osauga was playing with her children, and Hisse Watanabe was examining his watches on the second floor of the Loft department store in Sendai. She had come to Sendai for the day from Fukushima, which was one of the hardest-hit cities, on business.

When the earthquake hit, everyone fell down. The glass in the watch cases shattered. The panic rose in Watanable. Large pipes in the department store's ceiling began to come loose, swaying and banging into each other. It was if the whole building was coming apart by the earthquake.

The staff was calm and used to earthquakes. They told everyone to run outside despite the danger of falling debris.

Watanable ran out onto a walkway over the road. For some reason, there was a giant statute of the letter "P", poised at a funny angle. Everyone took pictures with their photo cameras.

Then the walkway started swaying badly, and they ran down the street. People screamed in the chaos. Watanable spent the rest of the day trying to find shelter, and ended up passing a cold, hungry night at a railway station. She was waiting to return home when the trains started running again. She didn't know she would have a long wait to get back home, as the trains were closed down.

As she talked, the petite, 30-year-old woman sat alone on a cardboard sheet in Sandai's city hall, crowed with refugees who had nowhere else to go. She appeared haggard and shell shocked.

Like Osauga, construction worker Yukou Ito was lucky enough to reach higher ground – barely Ito was at work about 40 minutes from his home near the harbor in Hachinohe when the earthquake struck. He returned in time to see a wall of rising water, which funneled cars and boats down the street toward him.

"It was terrifying. It looked like a foreign movie where everyone's running from something scary," he said.

Ito grabbed a credit card and jumped into his compact car. Through his rearview minor, he could see the huge tsunami crashing down the street just behind him. A fishing boat was right behind him.

Now, several inches (centimeters) of water cover the floor at the entrance of his apartment, along with his ruined refrigerator, his microwave and a cabinet. A pile of muddy clothes soak in a large plastic bucket filled with water.

"I have to start over from square one," he said, lighting a cigarette and looking at the men in hard hats who were dragging debris and twisted metal out of buildings. Huge fishing boats were turned on their sides in the road like children's toys. "I've got nothing left."

Still overcome by emotion, Imai paces back and forth along the Sunashi river that runs through his small hometown of Tagajo, and his knee-high wading boots scraping along the ground. Other dazed survivors roam the devastated streets.

As Imai remembers his older neighbors who likely died in their houses, he breaks into tears.

This river has given us much, but on Friday it brought disaster," said the 56 year-old, a former hotel worker who quit his job to care for his wife of 33 years. "Even now, when I sit or close my eyes, I still feel like it is shaking."

As he talked, the river current was switching directions and suddenly dropped several feet (a meter) – signs of another possible tsunami. A few minutes later came a small wave about a food (30 centimeters), carrying oddly shaped debris.

It spun and dipped as it slowly floated by.

CHAPTER SEVENTEEN

The 2011 earthquake and tsunami which occurred and it was 9.0 Mw megathrust earthquake off the coast of Japan, that occurred at 14.46 (05:46 UTC) on Friday 11th of March 2011.

The epicenter was reported to be 130 kilometers (81 mi) off the coast of the Oshika Peninsula, Tohoku, with the hypocenter at a depth of 32 km (20 mi).

It is known that the earthquake triggered tsunami warnings and evacuations along Japan's Pacific coast and in at least 20 countries, including the entire Pacific coast of North America and South America. The people in that area were warned but yet they weren't prepared to leave their homes in such a hurry, but that meant they would lose their lives if they didn't get to a higher ground.

The earthquake created extremely destructive tsunami waves of up to 10 meters (33 ft) that struck Japan minutes after the quake, and in some cases traveling up to 10 km (6 mi) inland, with smaller waves after several hours in many other countries. The people in that area had to run for their lives. They didn't expect such a quick reaction of the tsunami, but the tsunami was doing its job, washing that area clear of anything on it, people or houses. The whole situation was terrible and no one could stop the terror in their area. It was run for your lives or die on the spot and many persons were caught unaware by the tsunami and they didn't live to tell the tale.

The Japanese National Police Agency has officially confirmed that 3,373 deaths, 1,990 injuries and 7,558 people are missing across 16 prefectures, but estimated number were far higher, ranging from thousands to tens of thousands dead or missing. The earthquake and tsunami caused extensive and severe damage in Japan, including heavy damage to roads and railways as well as fires in many areas, and a dam collapse. Around 4.4 million households in northern Japan were left without electricity, and 1.4 million without water. Many electrical generators were taken down, and at least three nuclear reactors partly melt down, which prompted evacuations of the affected areas, and a state of emergency was established. The proper authorities knew the whole situation was not good, and radiation was in the air. They knew they had to do something to make the situation better, but that was easily said than done. They knew it would be a hard struggle to fix the three reactors. The reactors believed to have partially melted down would have experienced a chemical explosion extensively damaging their buildings. All this damage was caused by the tsunami, and the integrity of the inner core-containment vessel of one of the compromised, and some dangerous radioactive release from the plant has occurred.

Residents within a 20 km (12 mi) radius of the Fukushima 1 Nuclear Power Plant and a 10 km (6.2 mi) radius of the Fukushima II Nuclear Power Plant were evacuated. The people in that area had no idea what was happening. They felt they would just be away from their homes for a couple of weeks, but now they were told they could not go back to that area, because it was contaminated by radiation. They knew what that meant that they had lost everything they had in that area. They would have to start all over again and they wanted to be compensated. Early estimates from AIR Worldwide place insured losses from the earthquake alone at US$14.5 to $34.6 billion.

The Chief economist for Japan at Credit Suisse, Hiromichi Shirakawa, said in a note to clients that the estimated economic loss may be around $171-183 billion just to the region which was hit by the quake and tsunami. The Bank of Japan offered Y15 trillion (US$183 billion) to the banking system on the 14th of March 2011 to normalize market conditions.

The estimates of the Sendai earthquake's magnitude made it strongest known earthquake to hit Japan, and one of the five strongest earthquakes in the world over since modern record-keeping began in 1900. Japanese Prime Minister Naoto Kan said that "in the 65 years after the end of World War II, this is the toughest and most difficult crisis for Japan. The earthquake moved Honshu 2.4. m (7.9 ft) east and shifted the Earth on its axis by almost 10 cm (3.9 in).

Earthquake:

The main earthquake was preceded by a number of large foreshocks, beginning with a 7.2. Mw event on the 9th of March approximately 40 km (25 mi) from the 11th of March quake, and followed by another three on the same day in excess of 6 Mw in magnitude. One minute prior of the effects of the earthquake being felt in Tokyo, the Earthquake Early Warning system connected to more than 1,000 seismometers in Japan sent out warnings on the television of an impending earthquake to millions. This was possible because the damaging seismic S-waves, traveling at 4 kilometers per second, took about 90 seconds to travel the 373 km (232 mi) to Tokyo. The early warning was believed by the Japan Meteorological Agency to have saved many lives. But in theory the people were slow to comprehend what was on their door steps and they should run for their lives, but most didn't comprehend what was about to happen – their lives and their dreams would be gone forever.

The earthquake occurred at 14.46 on local time in the Western Pacific Ocean and at 130 km (81 mi) east of Sendai, Honshu, Japan. Its epicenter was 373 km (232 mi) from Tokyo, according to the United States Geological Survey (USGS). Multiple aftershocks were reported after the initial magnitude 9.0 quake. A magnitude 7.0 aftershock was reported at 15:06 local time, 7.4 at 15:15 local time and 7.2 at 15:26 local time. Over five hundreds aftershocks of magnitude 4.5 or greater have occurred since the initial quake.

Initially reported at 7.9 by the USGS, magnitude was quickly upgraded to 8.8 and then to 8.9, and then again to 9.0. This earthquake occurred where the Pacific is subduction under the plate beneath northern Honshu, which plate this was a matter of debate amongst scientists. The Pacific plate, which moves at a rate of 8 to 9 cm (3.1 to 3.5 in) a year, dips under Honshu's underlying plate releasing large amounts of energy. This motion pulled the upper plate down until it broke. The break 130 kilometers (81 mi) off of the coast of Sendai was estimated to be several tens of kilometers long and only 32 kilometers (20 mi) deep caused the sea floor to spring up several meters, causing the earthquake. A quake of this size usually has a rupture length of at least 480 km (300 mi) and requires a long, relatively straight fault line. Because the plate boundary and subduction zone in this region was not very straight, and it was unusual for the magnitude of an earthquake to exceeded 8.5, the magnitude of this earthquake was a surprise to some seismologists. The hypocentral region of the earthquake it extended from offshore Iwate to offshore Ibaraki Prefectures. The Japanese

Meteorological Agency said that the earthquake may have ruptured the fault zone from Iwate to Ibaraki where a length of 500 km (310 mi) and a width of 200 km (120 mi). Analysis showed that this earthquake consisted of a set of three events. The earthquake may have had a mechanism similar to that of another large earthquake in 1869 with estimated magnitude Ms 8.6, which also created a large tsunami. Other major earthquakes with tsunamis struck the Sanriku Coast in 1896 and 1933.

The quake registered the maximum of 7 on the Japan Meteorological Agency seismic intensity scale in Kurihara, Miyagi Prefecture. Three other prefectures – Fukushima, Ibaraki and Tochigi – recorded an upper 6 on the JMA scale. Seismic stations in Iwate, Gunma, Saitama and Chiba Prefecture measured a lower 6, recording an upper 5 in Tokyo.

Energy:

This earthquake released a surface energy (Ms) of 1.9+0.5x10 joules, dissipated as shaking and tsunami energy, which nearly doubled that of the 9.1- magnitude 2004 Sumatran earthquake that killed 230,000 people, and flung the 2,600 ton Apron 1 ship 2 to 3 km (1.2 to 1.9 mi) inland. "If we could only harness the (surface) energy from this earthquake, it would power (a) city the size of Los Angeles for an entire year," USGS director Marcia McNutt said in an interview. The total energy released (Mw) was more than 200,000 times the surface energy and was calculated by the USGS WPhase Moment Solution at 3.9x10 joules, slightly less than the 2004 Sumatra quake. This is equivalent to 9.32 tritons of TNT (approximately 600 million times that of the Hiroshima bomb, or 186,400 times as powerful as man's largest-ever explosive device, Tsar Bomba).

Geophysical Impact:

The quake moved portions of northeast Japan by as much as 8 ft (2.4 m) closer to North America, making portions of Japan's landmass "wider than before," according to geophysicist Ross Stein. Portions of Japan closest to the epicenter experienced the large shifts. Dr. Stein also noted that a 400 km (250 mile), allowing the tsunami to travel farther and faster onto land.

According to Italy's National Institute of Geophysics and Volcanology, and the earthquake's enormous strength shifted the Earth's axis by 25 centimeters (9.8 in). This deviation led to a number of small planetary changes, including the length of a day and the tilt of the Earth. The speed of the Earth's rotation increased, shortening the day by 1.8 microseconds due to the redistribution of Earth's mass.

Shinmoedake, a volcano in Kyushu, erupted two days after the earthquake. The volcano had erupted in January 2011 and it was not known if the later eruption was linked to the earthquake.

Tsunami:

The earthquake caused a massive tsunami which wrought massive destruction along the Pacific coastline of Japan's northern islands. The tsunami propagated across the Pacific, and warnings were issued and evacuations carried out in many countries with Pacific coasts, including the entire Pacific coast of North and South America from Alaska to Chile, however, while the tsunami was felt in many of these places, it caused only relatively minor effects. Chile has the Pacific coast furthest from Japan (about 17,000 km away – the furthest possible distance on the earth is the semi-circumference, about 20,000 km, but was still stuck by tsunami waves up to 2 meters high. Every country was taking the warning seriously, and were doing everything in their power to prevent any damage from the tsunami.

Japan:

The tsunami warning issued by the Japan Meteorological Agency was the most serious on its warning scale, and it rated as a "Major tsunami", being at least 3 m (9.8 ft) high. The actual height predicted varied, the greatest being for Miyagi at 10 m (33 ft) high. The earthquake took place at 14.46 JST around 70 km (43 mi) from the nearest point on Japan's coastline, and initial estimates indicated the tsunami would have taken 10 to 30 minutes to reach the areas first affected, and then areas further north and south based on the geography of the coastline. Just over an hour after the earthquake, a tsunami was observed at 15:55 JST flooding Sendai Airport, which is located near the coast of Miyagi Prefecture, with waves sweeping away cars and planes and flooding various buildings as they traveled inland. The impact of the tsunami in and around Sendai Airport was filmed by an NHK News helicopter, showing a number of vehicles on local roads trying to escape the approaching wave and being engulfed by it. A 4-meter (13 ft)-high tsunami hit Iwate Prefecture.

Like the 2004 Indian Ocean earthquake and tsunami and Cyclone Nargis, the damage by surging water, though much more localized, and was far more deadly and destructive than the actual quake. There were reports of "whole towns were gone" from tsunami-hit areas in Japan, including 9,500 missing in Minamisanriku, one thousand bodies had been recovered in the town by 14th of March 2011.

Kuji and Ofunato have been "swept away – leaving no trace that a town was there. Also destroyed was Rikuzentakata, where the tsunami was reportedly three stories high. Other cities reportedly destroyed or heavily damaged by the tsunami include Miyako, Otsuchi, and Yamada (all in Iwate Prefecture), Namie, Soma and Minamisoma (all in Fukushima Prefecture) and Onagawa, Natori, Ishinomaki, and Kesennuma (all in Miyagi Prefecture). The severest effects of the tsunami were felt along a 670-kilometer (420 mi)-long stretch of coastline from Erimo in the north to Oarai in the south, with most of the destruction in that area occurring in the hour following the earthquake.

On the 13th of March 2011, the Japan Meteorological Agency (JMA) published details of tsunami observations recorded around the coastline of Japan following the earthquake. These observations included tsunami maximum readings of over 3 meters (9.8 ft) at the following locations and times on the 11th of March 2011, following the earthquake at 14:46 JST.

15:12 JST – Iwate Kamaishi-oki – 6.8 m (22 ft).
15:15 JST – Ofunato – 3.2 m (10 ft) or more.
15:20 JST – Ishinomaki-shi Ayukawa – 3.3 m (11 ft) or more.
15:21 JST – Miyako – 4.0 m (13.1 ft) or more.
15:21 JST – Kamaishi – 4.1 m (13 ft) or more.
15:44 JST – Erimo-cho Shoya – 3.5 m (11 ft).
15:50 JST – Soma – 7.3 m (24 ft).
16:52 JST – Oarai – 4.2 m (14 ft).

These readings were obtained from recording stations maintained by the JMA around the coastline of Japan. Many areas were also affected by tsunamis of 1 to 3 meters (3.3 to 9.8 ft) in height, and the JMA bulletin also included the caveat that "At some parts of the coasts, tsunamis may be higher than those observed at the observation sites." The timing of the earliest recorded tsunami maximum readings ranged from 15:12 to 15:21, between 26 and 35 minutes after the earthquake had struck. The bulletin also included initial tsunami observation details, as well as more detailed maps for the coastlines affected by the tsunamis.

CHAPTER EIGHTEEN

Elsewhere Across the Pacific:

Shortly after the earthquake, the Pacific Tsunami Warning Center (PTWC) issued tsunami watches and warnings for locations in the Pacific. At 07:30 UTC PTWC issued a widespread tsunami warning for the entire Pacific Ocean. The United States West Coast and Alaska Tsunami Warning Center issued a tsunami warning for the coastal areas of California and Oregon from Conception, California, to the Oregon-Washington border. In California and Oregon, up to 8 ft (2.4 m) high tsunami surges hit some areas, damaging docks and harbors and causing over US$10 million of damage. Hawaii estimated damage to public infrastructure alone at $3 million. A tsunami warning was also advised for the Canadian province of British Columbia, where the potentially affected areas included British Columbia's north coast and the outer west coast of Vancouver Island.

Some South Pacific countries, including Tonga, American Samoa and New Zealand, experienced larger-than-normal waves, but did not report any major damage.

Along the Pacific Coast of Mexico and South America, tsunami surges were reported, but in most places caused little or no damage. Peru reported a wave of 1.5 meters (4.9 ft) and over 300 homes damaged. The surge in Chile was large enough to cause some damage.

Russia evacuated 11,000 residents from coastal areas of the Kuril Islands. In the Philippines, waves up to 0.5 meters (1.6 ft) high hit the eastern seaboard of the country.

Casualties:

Both the earthquake and the resultant tsunami caused many casualties. Unlike other countries which had many hours' notice of a relatively small surge, a major tsunami struck Japan with only minutes' warning, leaving many people unable to escape. They had no idea it would be their last days on earth, their dreams and all their earthly possessions would be washed away by a tsunami. This would be really their dreadful dream.

The National Police Agency has officially confirmed 3,373 people dead, 1,990 injured, and 7,558 missing across sixteen prefectures in Japan. These numbers were expected to significantly increased, with casualties expected to reach tens of thousands.

Prefectural officials and the Kyodo News Agency, quoting local officials, said that 9,500 people from Minamisanriku in Miyagi Prefecture – about a half of the town's population were unaccounted for. NHK has reported that the death toll in Iwate Prefecture alone may reach 10,000.

Officials in Wakabayashi-ku, Sendai, which heavily damage by tsunami waves, stated that they had found the bodies of 200-300 victims, who were washed up on the beach, and they had to be buried.

It was reported that four passenger trains containing an unknown number of passengers disappeared in a coastal area during the tsunami. One of the trains, on the Senseki Line, was found derailed in the morning and all the passengers were rescued by a police helicopter. Der Spiegel later reported that five missing trains in Miyagi Prefecture had been found with all passengers safe, although this information could not be confirmed locally.

By 9:30 UTC on March 111, Google Person Finder, which was previously used in the Haitian, Chilean, and Christchurch, New Zealand earthquakes, was collecting information above survivors and their locations. The Next of Kin Registry NOKR was assisting the Japanese government in locating next of kin for those missing or deceased.

One man was killed in Papua, Indonesia after being swept out to sea. Near Crescent City, California, a 25-year-old man who was said to have been attempting to photograph the oncoming tsunami was swept out to sea and confirmed dead.

Damage and effects:

The degree of damage caused by the earthquake and tsunami combined, most due to the tsunami, was very great. The film of the worst affected towns show nothing more than piles of rubble, with almost no parts of any structures left standing. The tsunami was such a great force that it took everything in its way, buildings or people or whatever stood in its way. The extent of the damage was also massive. Estimates of the value of the damage range into the tens of billions of US dollars, before and after satellite photographs of devastated regions show immense damage to many places. The dreams of the people were washed away by this powerful tsunami and also their lives were washed away, and they were no more to see the sun and day light of their great country.

Nuclear power plants:

Fukushima I, Fukushima II, Onagawa Nuclear Power Plant and Tokai nuclear power stations consisting of eleven reactors were automatically shut down following the earthquake. Higashidori, also on the northeast coast, was already shut down for a periodic inspection. Cooling was needed to remove decay heat for several days after a plant has been shut down for a periodic inspection. The cooling process was powered by emergency diesel generators, as in the case of Rokkasho nuclear reprocessing plant. At Fukushima I and II tsunami waves overtopped seawalls and destroyed diesel backup systems, leading to severe problems including two large explosions at Fukushima I and leakage of radiation. They now knew that it was dangerous for the people in that area and they had to evacuate over 200,000 people out of that area, because of radiation from the leaking power plant. This was really dangerous for the residents' health.

Seismic recording at six assessed nuclear power facilities indicated the plants had been exposed to peak ground accelerations of 0.0285-0.5324-g and peak ground velocities of: 4,127-67.3216 cm/sec.

Europe's energy commissioner Guenther Oettinger, in remarks to the European Parliament on the 15th of March, called the nuclear disaster an "apocalypse", saying that the word was particularly well chosen, and that Tokyo had almost lost control of events at the Fukushima power plant.

Fukushima I and II Nuclear Power Plants:

Japan declared a state of emergency following the failure of the cooling system at the Fukushima I Nuclear Power Plant, resulting in the evacuation of nearby residents. Officials from the Japanese Nuclear and Industrial Safety Agency have reported that radiation levels inside the plant were up to 1,000 times normal levels, and that levels outside the plant were up to 8 times normal levels. Later, a state of emergency was declared at the Fukushima II nuclear power plant about 11 km (7 mi) south. This brings the total number of problematic reactors to six, two which (unit 1 and 3 at Fukushima 1) experienced a partial meltdown.

All the residents in that area were bused away from that area, because it wasn't in their best interest to be there. They didn't understand what was happening, because they were told very little about the whole situation. The government didn't want them to know the real reason for the evacuation. The whole situation was serious. They had no idea when they would return to their homes, as they had to leave with just a tooth brush and their poor lives in their hands. The earthquake and the tsunami had taken over their whole lives and nothing would be the same again.

On March 12, a large explosion, thought to be caused by the buildup of hydrogen gas, blew away the roof and the outer walls of the Reactor I building a large cloud of dust and vapor, but the reactor itself was damaged in the explosion. A BBC journalist reported being stopped 60 km from the blast site by police. They knew the whole situation was serious and no one was allowed to be near that site. It was dangerous because of leaking radiation.

At 01:17 JST on Sunday 13th of March (12 March 16:17 GMT), the Japan Atomic Energy Agency announced that it was rating the Fukushima accident at 4 (accident with local consequences) on the 0-7 International Nuclear Event Scale (INES), below the Three Mile Island accident in seriousness. This has been questioned by the French ASN nuclear safety authority. They say the accident can be classed as a 5 or 6, which would be comparable to or worse than the Three Mile Island accident.

Another explosion occurred at Reactor 3 of the Fukushima I plant just after 11:00 a.m. local time on March 14. An exterior wall of the building collapsed, but the reactor vessel was not damage according to a government spokesperson. At 16:29 UTC on Monday 14 March (14 March 01:29 UTC), the Japanese Nuclear and Industrial Safety announced that the explosion had occurred. The local population was advised by the authorities to stay home until the radioactive situation of the environment was totally clarified. Unlike the other five reactors units, reactor 3 runs on mixed uranium and plutonium oxide, or MOX fuel, making it potentially more dangerous in an incident due to the neutronic effects of plutonium on the reactor and the carcinogenic effects in the event of release to the environment. Tokyo Electric Power Company (TEPCO) was trying to reduce the pressure within the plants by venting contaminated steam from the reactor vessels into the atmosphere. According to Tomoko Murakami, of the nuclear energy group at Japan's Institute of Energy Economics, this would not result in the release of significant radiation. Residents living within a 20 km (12 mi) radius of the Fukushima I were evacuated, as well as residents within 3 km (1.9 mi) of the Fukushima II plant.

Additionally, it was reported on 14th of March at 07:00 ETD that the fuel rods of Reactor 2 at the Fukushima I plant were now fully exposed, and a meltdown of the fuel rods, with the risk of damage to the reactor vessel and a possible radioactive leak, could not be ruled out. As of the 14th of March, about 160 people have been exposed to dangerous radiation levels near the power stations. One plant employee was killed while operating a crane, eight others have been injured. An additional eleven employees were injured when the Reactor 3 building exploded. Several people received some radiation doses.

On Tuesday, March 15, at 6:10 a.m. local time an explosion occurred at Reactor 2 of the Fukushima I plant. Radiation "exceeding the legal limit" was detected outside the plant. The government admitted it was "very probable" that the cores of Reactors 1, 2 and 3 experienced meltdown due to high temperatures. According to TEPCO, the plant's operator, the radiation level at 8:31 a.m. local time had risen to 9:217 millisieverts (mSv) per hour, more than eight times the exposure permitted by law per year. Later the Chief Cabinet Secretary Yukio Adano announced that according to Tokyo Electric Power Company, the hourly radiation at the nuclear plant site reached 400 mSv. A fourth Fukushima I, Reactor 4, was also rocked by explosion on March 15.

A US Navy relief group moved from the immediate area after its helicopters detected low-level radiation while returning to their aircraft carrier from a SAR mission, 160 km (100 miles) offshore. The flight absorbed the equivalent amount of earthbound background radiation for a month, in the span of about an hour.

CHAPTER NINETEEN

Onagawa Nuclear Power Plant:

A fire from the turbine section of the Onagawa Nuclear Power Plant following the earthquake was reported by Kyodo News. The blaze was in a building housing the turbine, which was sited separately from the plant's reactor, and was soon extinguished.

On the 13th of March the lowest-level state of emergency was declared regarding the Onagawa plant by TEPCO, as radioactivity readings temporarily exceeded allowed levels in the area of the plant. TEPCO stated this was due to radiation from the Fukushima I nuclear accidents and not from the Onagawa plant itself.

Tokai Nuclear Power Plant:

The number 2 reactor at Tokai Nuclear Power Plant was shut down automatically. On 14 March it was reported that a cooling system pump for this reactor had stopped working, but the Japan Atomic Power Company stated that there was a second operational pump and cooling was working, but that two of three diesel generators used to power the cooling system were out of order.

Port:

The effects of the quake included visible smoke rising from a building in the Port of Tokyo with parts of the port areas being flooded, including soil liquefaction in Tokyo Disneyland's car park.

Dam failure:

The Fujinuma irrigation dam in Sukagawa ruptured, causing flooding and washing away homes. No casualties have been counted, but people are missing.

Water:

At least 1.5 million households were reported to have lost access to water supplies.

Electricity:

According to Tohoku Electric, around 4.4 million households in northeastern Japan were left without electricity. Several nuclear and conventional power plants went offline after the earthquake. Rolling blackouts began on 14th of March due to power shortages caused by the earthquake. The Tokyo Electric Power Company, which normally provides approximately 40 GW of electricity, announced that it can currently provide only about 30 GW. This is because 40 percent of the electricity used in the greater Tokyo area is now supplied by reactors in the Niigata and Fukushima prefectures. Two of those reactors, the Fukushima Dai-ichi and Fukushima Dai-ni, were automatically taken offline when the first earthquake occurred and have sustained major damage related to the earthquake and subsequent tsunami. Rolling blackouts of three hours are expected to last until the end of April and will affect the Tokyo, Kanagawa, Shizuoka, Yamanashi, Chiba, Ibaraki, Saitama, Tochigi, and Gunma prefectures.

Oil:

A 220,000-barrel-per-day oil refinery of Cosmo Oil Company was set on fire by the quake at Ich-ihara, Chiba Prefecture, to the east of Tokyo. Major fires broke out elsewhere, such as in the city of Kesennuma.

In Sendai, a 145,000-barrel-per-day refinery owned by the largest refiner in Japan, JX Nippon Oil & Energy was also set ablaze by the quake. Workers were evacuated, but tsunami warnings hindered efforts to extinguish the fire until the 14th of March, when officials planned to do so.

Transport:

Japan's transport network suffered severe disruption. Many sections of Tohoku expressway serving northern Japan were damaged. All railway services were suspended in Tokyo, with an estimated 20,000 people stranded at major stations across the city. In the hours after the earthquake, some train services were resumed. Most Tokyo area train lines resumed full service by the next day-12 March. Twenty thousand stranded visitors spent the night of the 11-12 of March inside Tokyo Disneyland.

A tsunami wave was seen flooding Sendai at 15:55 JST, about 1 hour after the initial quake Narita and Haneda Airport both suspended operations after the quake, with most flights diverted to other airports for about 24 hours. Ten airliners bound for Narita were diverted to nearby Yokota Air Base.

Various train services around Japan were also canceled, with JR East suspending all services for the rest of the day. Four trains on coastal lines were reported as being out of contact with operations, one, a four-car train on the Senseki Line, was found to have derailed, and its occupants were rescued shortly after 8 a.m. the next morning. There had been derailments of Shinkansen bullet train services in and out of Tokyo, but their services were suspended. The Tokaido Shinkansen resumed limited service late in the day and was back to its normal schedule by the next day, while the Joetsu and Nagano Shinkansen resumed services late on the 12th of March, however, the Tohoku Shinkansen remained suspended, with visible damage to electrical poles and elevated spans, and the state of the line in harder-hit areas still difficult to ascertain. Services on the Tohoku Shinkansen partially resumed on the 15th of March, with one round-trip service per hour between Tokyo and Nasu-Shiobara.

The rolling blackouts brought on by the crises at the nuclear power plants in Fukushima later had a profound effect on the rail networks around Tokyo starting on the 14th of March railways began running trains at 10-20 minute intervals (normally 3-5 minutes), operating some lines only at rush hour, and completely shutting down others (notably, the Tokaido Main Line, Yokosuka Line, Sobu Main Line and Chuo-Sobu Line were all stopped for the day). This led to near-paralysis within the capital, with long lines at train stations and many people unable to come to work or get home. The people in those areas didn't realize that the situation was so serious, and it was really impossible for the trains to run normally. It was really a sad day for those persons who were trying their best to get to work or to go home. They should count their blessing that they were still alive and others in other areas were washed away by the tsunami.

Telecommunications:
Cellular and landline phone service suffered major disruptions in

the affected area. Internet services, however, were to a large extent able to reroute around the damage, and only a few websites were initially unreachable. Several Wi-Fi hotspot providers have reacted to the quake by providing free access to their networks. People weren't able to get in touch with other persons, family or a good friend, and this was really a bad situation. Everyone was on there own.

Sports:

The 2011 World Figure Skating Championships were scheduled to take place from 21027 of March at the Yoyogi National Gymnasium in Tokyo but the International Skating Union decided on the 14th of March to postpone the event, after the German team announced that it would follow recommendations not to travel to Japan. International Skating Union President Ottavio Cinquanta published a statement on the federation website on March 15, confirming the cancellation of the event. However, the possibility of re-scheduling remains, said the ISU chief. "The postponement of the event or alternatively the final cancellation is under evaluation.

Also on hold is the ISU Figure Skating World Team Trophy, scheduled for Yokohama on April 14-17. The ISU is waiting for guidance from the Japanese authorities on whether skating championships can be held. "It is understood that a postponement of the above-mentioned World Championships as well as the holding of the ISU World Team Trophy is subject to the confirmation by the competent Japanese authorities that the situation is back to normal conditions allowing the safe conduct of major ISU sports Events in the Tokyo area," says the ISU.

Economic impact:

The northern Tohoku region, which was most affected, accounts for about 8 percent of the country's gross domestic product as it has factories that make products such as cars and beer as well as energy infrastructure. The region has been experiencing a brain and economic drainage as young people leave the area. It includes the northern Miyagi prefecture, where Sendai is located, about 300 km (180 miles) northeast of Tokyo. The Miyagi area includes manufacturing and industrial zones with chemical and electronics plants. It is estimated that Miyagi accounts for 1.7% of Japan's gross domestic product.

The earthquake and tsunami have had significant immediate impacts on business such as Toyota, Nissan and Honda, who completely suspended auto production until 14th of March. Nippon Steel Corporation also suspended production, Toyo Tire & Rubber Company and Sumitomo Rubber Industries shuttered their tire and rubber production lines, while GS Yuasa closed its automotive battery production. This was expected to hinder supply available for automakers. Tokyo Electric Power Company, Toshiba, East Japan Railway Company and Shin-Etsu Chemical Company were suggested as the most vulnerable companies as a result of the earthquake. Sony also suspended production at all its plants in the area, while Fuji Heavy Industries discontinued production at most of its factories in the Gunma and the Tochigi Prefectures. Other factories suspending operations include Kirin Holdings, GlaxoSmithKline and Toyota amid power cuts. The factory shutdowns, power cuts and the consequent presumed impact on consumer confidence could hurt the national GDP for several months, although economist Michael Boskin predicts "only minimal impact on the Japanese economy overall."

On the 14th of March, the Bank of Japan, in an attempt to maintain market stability, injected 15 trillion yen into the money markets to assure financial stability amid a plunge in stocks and surge in credit risk. After it set up an emergency task force to ensure liquidity in the aftermath of the disaster, and the governor Masaaki Dhirakawa and the bank's board also enlarged a program to buy government bonds to exchange-traded funds to the tune of 10 trillion yen. The BOJ chief told reporters cash injections will continue as needed. However, following the further nuclear leaks, its actions were read by the market as insufficient despite 8 trillion yen being pumped into the market. On the 15th of March, the Topix index fell again marking a two-day plunge not seen since 1987 as Japan's default risk surged after Prime Minister Naoto Kan warned of further leaks from the damage nuclear power plant. Commodities were also significantly lower. Residents of Tokyo were also reported to have gone on a panic shopping spree as daily necessities were sought after and gasoline was stocked up with the increasing risk of nuclear radiation leaks.

The Chief Secretary Yukio Edano has said that Japan's government will convene on the 13th of March to gauge the economic effects of the catastrophe. He also told NHK Television that about 200 billion yen that was remaining from the budget for the concurrent fiscal year that would end on the 31st of March would be used to find the immediate recovery efforts. Additional measures could also hurt Japan's public debt (which is already the highest in the world). This additional spending could hurt demand for government bonds.

Some economic analysts consider that, ultimately, the catastrophe will improve Japan's economy, with increased job availability during restoration efforts. An analyst at JP Morgan Chase, citing the 1989 San Francisco earthquake and the 1994 Northridge earthquake, noted that natural disasters "do eventually boost output." An analyst at Societe Generale anticipated that Japan's economy will decline in March but will revive powerfully in subsequent months. After the Kobe earthquake, industrial output dropped 2.6%, but increased by 2.2% the next month, and 1% the following month. Japan's economy then accelerated substantially through the next two years, at more than its former rate. Others are of the opinion that the catastrophe will harm the economy. Some have argued that those who predict that the reconstruction effort could help Japan's economy fall into broken window fallacy.

Global financial impact:

In the immediate aftermath of the earthquake, Japan's Nikkei stock market index saw its futures slide 5% in after-market trading. The Bank said that they would do their utmost to ensure financial market stability. On Tuesday, March 15, news of rising radiation level caused the Nikkei to drop over 1,000 points or 10.6 % (16% for the week).

Other stock markets around the world were also affected, the German DAX 1.2% and fell to 6,978 points within minutes. Hong Kong's Hang Seng index fell by 1.8% while South Korea's Kospi index slumped by 1.3%. By the end of trading on Friday, the MSCI Asia Pacific Index had dropped by 1.8%. Major U.S. stock markets indexes rose between 0.7%. Oil prices also dropped as a result of the closure of Japanese refineries, despite the ongoing violence in Libya and expected demonstrations in Saudi Arabia. U.S. crude dropped as low as $99.01 from $100.08 by lunchtime, with Brent Crude falling $2.62 to $112.81. In Hong Kong Financial Secretary John Tsang warned investors to "take extra care" as the earthquake may have a short term impact on each of the local stock market's.

The share prices of the biggest reinsurance companies Munich Re and Swiss Reinsurance Company fell following the earthquake on speculation that they may face losses "somewhere in the $10 billion range even after certain costs were absorbed by Japan's primary insurances and the government.

Peter Bradford, a former member of the United States' Nuclear Regulatory Commission, said that the impact on the nuclear power plant was "obviously a significant setback for the so-called nuclear renaissance. The image of a nuclear power plant blowing up before your eyes on a television screen is a first.

CHAPTER TWENTY

Government response:

Prime Minister Naoto Kan announced the government has mobilized the Japanese Self-Defense Forces in various earthquake disaster zones. He asked the Japanese public to act calmly and tune into various media for updated information. He also reported numerous nuclear power plants have automatically shut down to prevent damage and radiation leaks. He also set up emergency headquarters in his office to coordinate the government response.

Kan promised his 100% cooperation in alleviating the situation. He declared that "the safety of Japan's citizen is the priority, and to save every possible life is current mission." He added that the defense force, police, rescue crew and individuals are currently working at full potential to mediate the situation, and called for more help from all over Japan. Evacuation shelters currently are facing a shortage of potable water, food, blankets and bathroom facilities, as the government arranges these necessities to be delivered to where they are needed as soon as possible, from various areas of Japan and abroad.

Dropping temperatures due to the disruption in electrical and gas lines caused further problems at shelters.

A Japanese urban search and rescue team in New Zealand following the 2011 Christchurch earthquake was recalled.

Request for international assistance:

Japan specifically requested teams from Australia, New Zealand, South Korea, the United Kingdom, and the United States, it also requested, via its space agency JAXA, the activation of the International Charter on Space and Major Disasters, allowing diverse satellite imagery of affected regions to be readily shared with rescue and aid organization.

International response:

Among several resources offered to help find earthquake survivors and obtain information about people in Japan are: Disaster Message Board Web 171 operated by Nippon Telegraph and Telephone, the International Committee of the Red Cross, American Red Cross, Google Person Finder, websites of the Australian Embassy, U.S. Department of State. It was the UK Foreign and Commonwealth Office, and the Honshu Quake wiki operated by the Crisis Commons volunteer community.

Media coverage:

Japan's national public broadcast, NHK, and Japan Satellite Television suspended their usual programming to provide ongoing coverage of the situation. Various other nationwide Japanese TV networks also broadcast uninterrupted coverage of the disaster. Upstream Asia broadcast live feeds of NHK, Tokyo Broadcasting System, Fuji TV, TV Asahi, TV Kanagawa, and CNN on the Internet starting on the 12th of March 2011.

On the 14 of March, NHK News reported a Japan Meteorological Agency warning that was a 70% probability of a new earthquake exceeding magnitude 7.0 occurring within or near the same hypocentral region in the following three days.

Scientific and research response:

According to the chief scientist for the Multi-Hazards project at the U.S. Geological Survey, the fact that the Sendai earthquake took place in Japan – a country with "the best seismic information in the world" – meant that for the first time it was hoped that data had been collected that would allow modeling of an earthquake of this type and severity in great detail. Andreas Reitbrock, a professor of seismology at the University of Liverpool, agreed, stating that "It gives us, for the first time, the possibility to model in great detail what happened during the rupture of an earthquake.

The effect of this data is expected to be felt across other disciplines as well. Tom Heaton, a seismological engineer, commented that "the tragedy would provide unprecedented information about how buildings hold up under long periods of shaking and thus how to build them better. We had very little information about that before now.

CHAPTER TWENTY-ONE

The 2011 Tohaku earthquake and tsunami. Tohoku Chiho Taiheiyo-iki Jishin. literally. " Tohoku region Pacific Ocean offshore earthquake was caused by a 9.0-magnitude undersea megathrust earthquake off the coast of Japan that occurred at 14:46 JST (05:46 UTC) on Friday, 11 March 2011. The epicenter was approximately 72 kilometers (45 mi) east of the Oshika Peninsula of Tohoku, with the hypocenter at an underwater depth of approximately 32 km (19.9 mi).

The earthquake triggered destructive tsunami waves up to 30 m (98 ft) that struck Japan minutes after the quake, in some cases traveling up to 10 km (6 mi) inland, with smaller waves reaching many other countries after several hours. Tsunami warnings were issued and evacuations ordered along Japan's Pacific coast and at least 20 other countries, including the entire Pacific coast of North America and South America.

The Japanese National Police Agency has officially confirmed 11,362 deaths, and 2,872 injured, and 16,290 people missing across eighteen prefectures, as well as over 125, 000 buildings damaged or destroyed. The earthquake and tsunami caused extensive and severe structural damage in Japan, including heavy damage to roads and railways as well as fires in many areas, and a dam collapse. Around 4.4 million households in northeastern Japan were left without electricity and 1.5 million without water. Many electrical generators were taken down, and at least three nuclear reactors suffered explosions due to hydrogen gas that had build up within their outer containment buildings after cooling system failure. On 18 March, Yukija Amano – the head of the International Atomic Energy Agency described the crisis as "extremely serious." Residents within a 20 km (12 mi) radius of the Fukushima I Nuclear Power Plant and a 10 km (6 mi) radius of the Fukushima II Nuclear Power Plant were evacuated. Estimates of the Tohoku earthquake's magnitude make it the most powerful known earthquake to have hit Japan, and one of the five most powerful earthquakes in the world overall since modern record-keeping began in 1900. The Japanese Prime Minister Naoto Kan said, "In the 65 years after the end of World War II, this is the toughest and most difficult crisis for Japan. The earthquake moved Honshu 2.4 (7.9 ft) east and shifted the Earth on its axis by almost 10 cm (3.9 in). Early estimates placed insured losses from the earthquake alone at US$14.5 to $34.6 billion. The Bank of Japan offered Y15 trillion (US$183 billion) to the banking system on 14 March in an effort to normalized market conditions. On 21 March, the World Bank estimated damage between US$122 billion and $235 billion. Japan's government said the cost of the earthquake and tsunami that devastated the northeast could reach $309 billion, making it the world's most expensive natural disaster on record.

Earthquake:

The 9.0-magnitude (Mw) undersea megathrust earthquake occurred on 11 March 2011 at 14:46 JST in the western Pacific Ocean, with its epicenter approximately 72 kilometers (45 mi) east of the Oshika Peninsula of Tohoku, Japan, lasting approximately six minutes. The nearest major city to the quake was Sendai, Honshu, Japan, 130 km (81 mi) away. The quake occurred 373 km (232 mi) from Tokyo. The main earthquake was preceded by a number of large foreshocks, and multiple aftershocks were reported afterwards. The first major foreshock was a 7.2 Mw event on 9 March, approximately 40 km (25 mi) from the location of the 11 March quake, with another three on the same day in excess of 6.0 MW. Following the quake, a 7.0 aftershock was reported at 15:06 JST, followed by a 7.4 at 15:15 and a 7.2 at 15:26 JST. Over six hundred aftershocks of magnitude 4.5 or greater have occurred since the initial quake. The United States Geological Survey (USGS) director Marcia McNutt explained that aftershocks follow Omori's Law, might continue for years, and will taper off in time.

CHAPTER TWENTY-TWO

Manufacturing in Japan:

Japan's major export industries include automobiles, consumer electronics, computers, semiconductors, copper and iron and steel.

Additional key industries in Japan's economy are petrochemicals, pharmaceuticals, bioindustry, shipbuilding, aerospace, textiles, and processed foods.

Japanese manufacturing industry is heavily dependent on imported raw materials and fuel.

Shipbuilding:

Japan dominated world shipbuilding in the late 1980s, filling more than half of all orders worldwide. Its closest competitors were South Korea and Spain, with 9% and 5.2% of the market, respectively.

The Japanese shipbuilding industry was hit by a lengthy recession from the late 1970s through most of the 1980s, which resulted in a drastic cutback in the use of facilities and in the work force, but there was a sharp revival in 1989. The industry was helped by a sudden rise in demand from other countries that needed to replace their aging fleet and from a sudden decline in the South Korean shipping industry. In 1988, Japanese shipbuilding firms received orders for 4.8 million gross tons of ships, but this figure grew to 7.1 million gross tons in 1989.

Although facing competition from South Korea and China, Japan retains a successful, advanced shipbuilding manufacturing industry.

Japan lost its position in the industry to South Korea in 2004, and its market share has since fallen sharply. The entire European countries' total market share has fallen to only a tenth of South Korea's, and the outputs of the United States and other countries have become negligible. Military shipbuilding s still dominated by US and European companies.

Aerospace:

The aerospace industry received a major boost in 1969 with the establishment of the National Space Development Agency (now Japan Aerospace Exploration Agency), which was changed with the development of satellites and lunch vehicles.

The Japanese military industry, although a small share of GDP, is a major sector of the economy. It is technologically advanced and is very successful, and has produced such aircraft as the new Mitsubishi fighter planned to be launched.

Petrochemicals:

The petrochemical industry experienced moderate growth in the late 1980s because of steady economic expansion. The highest growth came in the production of plastics, polystyrene, and polypropylene. Prices for petrochemicals remained high because of increased demand in the newly developing doggie economies of Asia.

By 1990, the construction of factory complexes to make ethylene-based products in the South Korea and Thailand was expected to increase supplies and reduce prices. In the long term, the Japanese petrochemical industry is likely to face intensifying competition as a result of the integration of domestic and international markets and the efforts made by other Asian countries to catch up with Japan.

Biotechnology and pharmaceutics:

The biotechnology and pharmaceutical industries experienced strong growth in the late 1980s. Pharmaceutical production grew an estimated 8% in 1989 because of increased expenditures by Japan's rapidly aging population. Leading producers actively developed new drugs, such as those for degenerative and geriatric disease. Pharmaceutical companies were establishing tripolar networks connecting Japan, the United States, and Western Europe to co-ordinate product development. They also increased merger and acquisition activity overseas. Biotechnology projects, with full-scale commercialization expected to take place in 1990s.

Biotechnology research covered a wide variety of fields: agriculture, animal husbandry, pharmaceuticals, chemicals, food processing, and fermentation. Human hormones and proteins for pharmaceutical products were sought through genetic recombination using bacteria.

Biotechnology also is used to enhance bacterial enzyme properties to further improve amino-acid fermentation technology, a field in which Japan is the world leader. The government cautions Japanese producers, however, against over optimism regarding biotechnology and bioindustry. The research race both in Japan and abroad intensified in the 1980s, leading to patent disputes and forcing some companies to abandon research. Also, researchers began to realize that such development continually showed complexities, requiring more technical breakthroughs than first imagined. Yet, despite these problems, research and development was still expected to be successful and to end in product commercialization in the mid-term.

In 2006, the Japanese pharmaceutical market was the second largest individual market in the world. With sales of $60 billion it constitutes approximately 11% of the world market.

The Japanese Pharmaceutical Industry and Laws are very particular. They are ruled by The Ministry of Health, Labor, and Welfare which was established by a merger of the Ministry of Health and Welfare and the Ministry of Labor, on January 6, 2001 as part of the Japanese government program for re-organizing government ministries.

Motor vehicle and machinery:

Japanese global motor vehicle companies are:

Toyota	Lexus
Hino	Daihatsu
Honda	Acura
Nissan	Infiniti
Suzuki	Mazda
Mitsubishi	Subaru
Isuzu	

And Denso is the world largest company in automotive components manufacturer. In addition Honda, Suzuki, Yamaha and Kawasaki are global motorcycle companies.

The motor vehicle industry is one of the most successful industries in

Japan, with large world shares in automobile, electrical machineries, parts, Tire and engine manufacturing.

Japan is home to six of the top 10 largest vehicle manufacturers in the world. For example it is home to multinational companies such as Toyota, Honda, Nissan, Suzuki and Mazda. Some of these companies cross-over to different sectors such as electronics to produce electronic equipment as some of them being a part of keiretsu. Japan's automobiles are generally known for their quality, durability, fuel efficiency and more features for a relatively cheaper price than competitors.

Japan car makers, Mitsubishi and Toyota, have had their patents violated by Myanmar car makers, such as UD Group (Mandalay), Kyar Koe Kaung (Yangon). These Myanmar car makers produced Mitsubishi and Toyota products including Mitsubishi Pajero, Toyota Town ace pick up and other various types of Japanese car under their owned tradename (Khit Tayar Pajero, Shwe Surf, UD Light Truck and KKK Light Truck).

Export and Japanese market:

In 1991, Japan produced 9.7 million automobiles, making it the largest producer in the world, and in the United States in that year produced 5.4 million. It was just under 46% of the Japanese output was exported. Automobiles, other motor vehicles, and automotive parts were the largest class of Japanese exports throughout the 1980s. In 1991 they accounted for 17% of all Japanese exports, a meteoric rise from only 1.9% in 1960 with kaya one of the largest exporters.

Fear of protectionism in the United States led to major foreign investments in the USA by Japanese automobile manufacturers. By the end of the 1980s, all the major Japanese producers had automotive assembly lines operating in the United States: Isuzu has a joint plant with Subaru, and one of Toyota's plants is in Alabama. Following the major assembly firms, Japanese producers of automobile parts also began investing in the United States in the late 1980s. Most Japanese auto parts are still made in Japan.

Automobiles were a major area of contention for the Japan-United States relationship during the 1980s. When the price of oil rose in the 1979 energy crisis, demand for small automobiles increased, which worked to the advantage of Japan's exports to the United States market. As the Japanese share of the market increased, to 21.8% in 1981, pressure rose to restrict imports from Japan. The result of these pressures was a series of negotiations in early 1981, which produced a voluntary export agreement limiting Japan's shipments to the United States to 1.68 million units (excluding certain kinds of specialty vehicles and trucks). This agreement remained in effect for the rest of the decade, but Japanese competition only increased with new plants being built and with the export agreement being voluntary.

Similar voluntary restraints on Japanese exports were imposed by Canada and several West European countries. Nonetheless, Japanese car competition only increased due to new plants being built and with the export agreements being voluntary. Since then, tensions have greatly decreased. It was Canada and Western Europe, like the U.S., repealed restrictions on Japanese auto imports. Nissan has a assembly plant in Sunderland in England.

Imports:

Foreign penetration of the automotive market in Japan has been less successful. Imports of foreign automobiles were very low during the forty years prior to 1985, never exceeding 60,000 units annually or 1% of the domestic market. Trade and investment barriers restricted imported automobiles to an insignificant share of the market in the 1950s, and as barriers were finally lowered, strong control over the distribution networks made penetration difficult. The major United States automobile manufacturers acquired minority interest in some Japanese firms when investment restrictions were relaxed, Ford obtained a 25% interest in Toyota Kogyo (Mazda), General Motors a 34% interest in Isuzu, and Chrysler a 15% interest in Mitsubishi Motors. This ownership did not provide a means for United States automobiles to penetrate the Japanese market, and the American car companies eventually got rid of their shares of the Japanese carmakers.

After the strong appreciation of the yen in 1985, however, Japanese demanded for foreign automobiles increased, but with most cars being from Germany. In 1988, automobile imports totalled 150,629 units, of which 127,309 were European, mostly German. Only 21,124 units were imported from the United States at that time.

Electronics:

Many of the world's major electronics companies are based in Japan, including:

Canon	Citizen	Fujitsu
Hitachi	Keyence	Mitsubishi Electric
NEC	Nikon	Nintendo
Panasonic	Sharp	Sega
Seiko	Sony	Toshiba
Yamaha		

Japan has 7 out of top 20 world's largest chip manufacturers as of 2005. Japan's electronic products are known for their quality, durability, and technological sophistication. Some of these companies cross over to automobile and finance sectors as part of a keiretsu.

Japan's computer industry developed with extraordinary speed and moved into international markets. Japanese computer technologies are some of the most advanced in the world.

The leading computer main frame manufacturers in Japan at the end of the 1980s (in the domestic market) were:

Fujitsu	Hitachi
NRC	IBM Japan
Unisys	

Leading personal computer manufacturers were:

NEC	Fujitsu
Seiko Epson	Toshiba
IBM Japan	

In 1988, Japan exported US $1.5 billion of computer equipment, up more than twelve fold from the US$122 million in 1980. Japanese firms were not successful in exporting mainframe computers, but they did very well in peripheral equipment, such as printers and tapes drives. In the rapidly growing personal computer markets, Japan achieved a major market share in the United States during the 1980s. Imports of computer equipment in 1988 came to US$3.2 billion (including parts).

Economic developments, namely outsourcing and globalization made these disputes obsolete by the 1990s. Japanese and U.S. influence in the computer market dwindled, with Taiwanese and mainland Chinese companies taking over component production and later research and development.

Food:

The production value of the food industry ranked third among manufacturing industries after electric and transport machinery. Japan produces a great variety of products, raging from traditional Japanese items, such as soybean paste (miso) and soy sauce, to beer and meat.

The industry as a whole experienced mild growth in the 1980s, primarily from the development of such new products as "dry beer" and precooked food, which was increasingly used because of the tendency of family members to dine separately and the trend toward smaller families, and convenience.

A common feature of all sectors of the food industry was their internationalization. As domestic raw materials lost their price competitiveness following the liberalization of imports, food makers more often produced foodstuffs overseas, promoted tie0ups with overseas firms, and purchased overseas firms.

In 2004, the Japanese food industry was worth US$600 billion whilst food processing was worth US$209 billion. This is comparable to the food industries of the United States and the EU.

CHAPTER TWENTY-THREE

Fishing Halted in Japan's Ibaraki after Radioactive Water Contaminates Sea:

Fishermen in Ibaraki preference, Japan's fifth-largest seafood producer halted operations after tainted fish were detected south of Fukushima, where radioactive water from a stricken nuclear plant contaminated the sea in that area.

About 96 percent of fishing off Ibaraki was suspended after sand lance contaminated with higher-than acceptable levels of cesium were discovered yesterday, said Tomoki Mashiko, assistant director at the fishing policy division of the government of prefecture. Fishing in Ibaraki had been suspended since the March 11 earthquake and tsunami, restarted as early as March 28, and then suspended again today.

Sushi restaurants and hotels, including Shangri-La Asia's Luxury chain, dropped Japanese seafood from their menus because of radiation fears. Japan exported 565,295 metric tons of marine products worth 195 billion yen ($2.3 billion) last year. A fishing industry group in Fukushima asked Tokyo Electric Co. to stop dumping toxic water into the sea as the operator of the damaged nuclear plant struggles to stem radiation leakage.

"The action may be undermining the whole fishing industry in Japan," Ikuhiro Hattori, chairman for the National Federation of Fisheries Co-Operative Association, told a vice trade minister today, referring to Tepco dumping water.

Fishermen Compensation:

The direction of tainted sand lance dealt a blow to Ibaraki fishermen who were recovering from the natural disaster and were resuming operations, Mashiko said. The prefecture produced 191,010 tons of fish worth 20 billion yen ($234 million) in 2008, representing 3.4 percent of Japan's output, government data shows.

Fishermen from Ibaraki's southern port of Hasaki weren't allowed to ship their products to market in neighboring Chiba prefecture, Mashiko said.

"We expect Tokyo Electric to treat fishermen the same way as it prepares to compensate farmers for their loss sales because of radioactive contamination," Mashiko said in an interview today. The prefecture will increase monitoring of marine products for radioactivity and decide which area and what type of fish are safe for commercial operations, he said.

Japan has restricted vegetable and raw milk shipments from Fukushima and nearby prefectures after discovering contamination products through random testing.

Tepco, owner of the nuclear plant hit by Japan's biggest quake on record, slumped as much as 19 percent to a record low today. The utility may make a preliminary compensation payment of 1 million yen ($12,000) to each household near its crippled Fukushima Dai-Ichi power plant Kyodo News reported.

Shifting Demand:

The cesium level detected samples of sand lance caught off the coast of Ibaraki was 526 becquerel per kilogram, and it was higher than Japan's health ministry standard of 500 becquerel, data from the prefecture showed yesterday.

Testing of sand-lance samples from fishermen's group in the northern town of Hirakata also showed they contained 4,080 becquerel per kilogram of iodine-131. The government set a radioactive iodine standard for fish at 2,000 becquerel per kilogram yesterday and the same as the limit for vegetables.

"Increased discovery of contaminated foods sapped consumer appetite for products made in Fukushima and surrounding areas," said Takaki Shigemoto, commodity analyst at JSC Corp. in Tokyo. "Demand is shifting from western Japan and overseas."

India suspended import of food from Japan for three months or until "credible information" on the radiation hazard is available, the health ministry said yesterday.

Exports of Japanese seafood were canceled by foreign buyers on concern the products may have been tainted by radiation leaking from the nuclear plant, Hiromi Isa, trade office director at Japan's Fisheries Agency, said last week.

Japan's total output of marine products reached 5.43 million tons in 2009. Fishing by Fukushima and nearby Miyagi prefectures remain suspended as they have recovered from damage caused by the quake and tsunami, according to the agency.

CHAPTER TWENTY-FOUR

Japan's quake:

At a factory owned by Furukawa Electric, just south of Tokyo, workers were trying to make the most of the electric they got.

That meant working night shifts and Saturdays.

"Cable manufacturing requires continuous electric, so rolling blackouts affect the residents badly," said Shinji Taniguchi, production manager of the factory.

"So we increased the number of our employees who work at night when there are no power cuts."

Demand for electric cables has risen since the devastating earthquake and tsunami struck on the 11 of March 2011.

They are used in everything from cars to planes to construction sites – including the reconstruction of the quake-hit areas.

"As a manufacturer of electric cables, we can only play a minor role, but we want to help bring the light back to the Tohoku area," Mr. Taniguchi said.

However, electric is not the only crucial ingredient that they have been struggling to get hold of.

"Our big concern is how to secure raw materials, because we used to get them from Fukushima," said Mr. Taniguchi.

"We had to look for alternative suppliers in other parts of Japan or from overseas. Now everyone is fighting over limited resources."

"But we have a responsibility to supply electric cables so we are doing as best as we can," he added.

No more blackouts:

The power cuts have been extremely unpopular among businesses.

So the government is asking major power users, such as factories and to cut their peak consumption by a quarter.

Without these cuts, demand for electricity could outstrip depleted supplies by the summer.

The president of Furukawa Electric, Masao Yoshida, is also the chairman of the Japanese Electric Wire and Cable Makers Association.

He says the new plan at least gives his industry certainty.

"It is definitely good news that there won't be any more rolling blackouts," Mr. Yoshida said.

But can Japan's factories maintain full productivity with 75% of electricity that they got before the quake?

"It will be tough," said Mr. Yoshida. "But this is an unprecedented disaster so we have to share the burden."

"We have three months to prepare before demand for electricity skyrockets in summer. I am sure we can all work together to save enough energy," he added.

Over the past month, words such as cooperation and unity have been repeated by many business leaders and politicians.

The people's attitude towards sharing the pain of the survivors of the earthquake and tsunami has been evident.

But one month on, Japan's period of mourning is coming to an end.

As the Japanese celebrate the start of spring, the mood of self-restraint, or jishuku, is giving way to the spirit of Japan."

People are coming together to help rebuild the Tohoku area.

If the price is a change in lifestyle or business practices, it seems that a price many Japanese households and firms are willing to pay.

Five-year power shortages:

But for how long does Japan need to live with less electricity? Or would it be until the summer? For six months? Or would it be until the end of the year?

"I expect electricity shortages to last for three to five years," said the country's economic minister, Kaoru Yossano.

"During that time, we need to make sure that productivity of factories doesn't drop, because the manufacturing sector is crucial to Japan's economic growth," he added.

Mr. Yossano said the Japanese people would have to save energy at home, as he recalled what he had to endure in the past.

"When I was a child, there were only two light bulbs at each household. No fridge, no air-condition," he said.

That may be slightly extreme, but the minister urges people to renew their old appliances or keep early hours.

"The Japanese people are wise, so if we explain clearly, I am confident they will cooperate," the minister added.

'Safer country':

But as residents of this rich nation used to life without so many neon signs, public anger towards nuclear power generator Tokyo Electric has been growing.

On Sunday, one of the biggest anti-nuclear protests took place all over Japan. In Koenji, Tokyo's residential area, several thousand people participated.

"This is the first protest that I have attended," said Sanae Takeshita.

"But I am here because I think we should get rid of nuclear energy. We should focus less on being one of the biggest economies in the world and focus on having a safer country," she added.

So will Japan be relying less on nuclear energy?

"Nuclear power remains an important source of energy," said Mr. Yosano. "This disaster will not change that because Japan does not have any natural resources."

Japan currently gets a quarter of its electricity from nuclear power plants.

"Whether we plan to rely on it less, I think we should not have the debate until things settle down and people regain their calmness," Mr. Yosano said.

He may be hoping that it will not take too long to regain people's trust in nuclear energy.

But footage of the ongoing battle at the Fukushima nuclear power plant was way too powerful for people to forget in the immediate future.

Nuclear energy is a way of the future, and the businesses of Japan depend on their nuclear power, and that is what make them so great in their industries, and they became one of the richest nations' in the world, and no one can stop they from their great dream of being one of the greatest nation's in the world.

CHAPTER TWENTY-FIVE

Japan's Prime Minister Naoto Kan Survives No-Confidence Vote:
Naoto Kan, widely unpopular for the handling of the nation's response to March earthquake and nuclear disaster, cuts a deal that blunts opposition and gives him more time.

Prime Minister Naoto Kan, right, and members of the Cabinet bow after a no-confidence motion was voted down in the Diet (Everett Brown /EPA / June 2, 2011.

It was the voting to stay in office only a few more months to guide the response to the nation's ongoing nuclear crisis, Japanese Prime Minister Naoto Kan on Thursday survived a parliamentary no-confidence vote aimed at driving him from power.

Kan, who assumed his job about a year ago and a cut and backroom political deal with members of the ruling Democratic Party of Japan only hours before parliamentary vote was to take place.

"I want the younger generation to take over my duties after I fulfill the role I should play in handling the disaster," a somber Kan told legislators.

The Prime Minister Kan said he needed time to help rebuild the nation after the March 11 earthquake and tsunami that struck northeastern Japan, leaving 23,000 people dead or missing and causing a major meltdown at the Fukushima Daiichi nuclear plant.

The final tally of the no-confidence vote, sponsored by the opposition Liberal Democratic Party, was 293 against ousting Kan and 152 supporting the move.

Still, Kan's critics say the lame-duck prime minister will be unable to inspire any consensus in a divided parliament, and Kan needs to pass an extra budget to pay for the mammoth rebuilding effort that lies ahead. He is also expected to make little headway in forging reform on taxes and social security, which many say is necessary to rein in the country's runway public debt.

Kan did not offer a firm date on when he would tender his resignation. But his predecessor, Yukio Hatoyama, told lawmakers earlier in the day that he supported Kan's plan to step down after negotiating the rebuilding budget – a job that probably could be accomplished by late summer.

Hatoyama had earlier backed the no-confidence motion. His about-face appeared to save the day for Kan, whose popularity has plummeted and who has been accused of botching the response by the crisis at the Fukushima Daiichi plant.

A new survey by the Pew Research Center's Global Attitudes Projects, which pulled 700 households in mid-April, and found that only 20% of Japanese residents believed that Kan's, or the Central Government had responded well to the crisis.

Many believed that Japanese voters are willing to give Kan more time because although they might opt for new leadership, they don't want to come in the middle of the rebuilding effort.

Such no-confidence votes are common in Japan, which has seen six different ministers in the last five years alone. Had the motion passed, Kan would have been required to leave office within 10 days. It was Kan's one year anniversary since taking office in June 8. It was unfortunate that the Japanese Government had this non-confidence vote, and throwing out each Prime Minister as it will, is certainly a very loyal political figure of the government and he is loyal to all of his fans. We find it a very terrible way to run a Government or a Prime Minister, who stood in the hands of the Government. It is stated that the Prime Minister resigned in August 2011 for reasons stated below.

Tokyo, Japan – the Japanese Prime Minister Naoto Kan, whose approval rating tumbled following the devastating March earthquake and tsunami, announced his resignation on Friday 26th of August 2011.

Kan announced he is stepping down as party leader during a meeting with members of the ruling Democratic Party of Japan. The party will elect a new leader next week, who will take over as prime minister.

The resignation fulfills his promise to step down after parliament approved two pieces of legislation, including one related to post-earthquake reconstruction.

"I will put my words into action once those two bills are approved," Kan said this month at a Lower House committee session.

Kan believes the two bills – the deficit-financing bond bill and the new energy promotion bill – will push forward his reconstruction policies.

The bills passed on Friday 26th of August 2011.

Kan has been under pressure to resign since the March 11 earthquake and tsunami and subsequent nuclear crisis in the nation. The disaster triggered the worst nuclear crisis since Chemobyl, as cores overheated and spewed radioactive material into surrounding areas.

Soon after the disaster, ratings agency Moody's put the country debt under review for a possible downgrade, as political infighting undermined measures to fix the budget deficit. Moody's officially downgraded Japan's credit on Wednesday, citing its unstable politics.

In June, the embattled leader narrowly escaped a vote of no confidence in parliament.

As many as nine candidates, including Finance Minister Yoshihiko Noda and former foreign minister, Seiji Maehara, are considered possible contenders for the post of prime minister.

Kan's resignation allows him to remain in office until the ruling party elects its new leader, a move scheduled for Monday 29th of August 2011.

A day later, parliament will vote in the new leader as prime minister, the sixth premier for the nation in five years.

Japan's next prime minister will inherit a series of problems, including soaring debt, nuclear woes, a shrinking population and nation struggling to rebuild after the devastating earthquake and tsunami.

CHAPTER TWENTY-SIX

I didn't know anything about the Japanese people, their dreams, and their destiny. I knew I had to use what I was born with. I remember what my mother, Edna, used to tell me, when I was a little boy growing up in British Guiana.

"You are my special boy," she would say.

"Why do you say I am special?" I asked. Because at that moment of time, I knew that everyone was special. But my mother saw something in me that I couldn't see in myself. She saw something that was entirely different in me, and only she could see my theory.

"Because you are my special child!" My mother would tell me.

"But everyone is special," I would tell her.

"Yes, but you are extra special." When she said extra special, I didn't understand the term, because I was still a little boy, who was really trying to understand my mother's advice.

"Why am I extra special?" I would ask curiously.

"Because you can hear things, see things, and most of all, you can feel things," she would explain. I didn't understand fully what my mother was trying to tell me, but I felt she was just trying to make me feel good, but that was a big mistake. My mother was right. She had told me the truth about myself. I had to put some of those technical skills that I had in me into operation, if I was going to write about some thing I knew very little about. I had it in me to go after what I wanted to write.

So, I was going to write about the Japanese people whom I knew very little about. I knew at the time I had to use some of my technical skills that I had in me. Only then I would get to know the whole situation that

I saw on TV, newspapers and the internet, but to really get to know those wonderful people of Japan, I would have to go back in time and see and to meet some of the Japanese people for myself and only then I would be able to finish this dramatic story of life and death on paper. It would be a dramatic story of life and death.

Here is where I cast my imagination to the nation of Japan. I found the modern Japanese people are very friendly, and they follow a modern tradition. They have the strength to help themselves and their families and also their beloved friends. They are also very religious and their religion is Buddhist, and most of all, they are hard working.

I can see it on their faces that they have to rebuild their towns and villages that were destroyed by the tsunami on the 11th of March 2011. Their hopes and their dreams were taken away by the dreadful storm. But their lives won't be the same – it would take a different turn for the best and they would have to a wait for the next calamity to happen, because their island of Japan was in the way of the dreadful earthquakes.

I didn't know how they got rid of their dead, and at that moment of time, I found out what was their religious beneficial way. They would cremate their dead. That was their religious way of life, and they would grieve and life would go on, so they would have to live to their grace and their dreams would be there to start new lives – lives for the future. Bless them all!

I hope you'll read my dramatic story of the Japanese people and their struggles in the land of Japan. I wish you'll tell your friends of this dramatic story, and you'll also read this book of love and laughter. Tell your friends and let them read it too. Bless you all!

About the Author

Frank Senauth was born in Guyana, South America. He worked in London, England. Then in 1973 he emigrated to Canada. He felt that Canada held better prospects for him. He worked at several jobs until he was able to start his own business.

In 1986, he retired from his business and return to his boyhood dream of becoming a writer. Having the leisure to pursue a writing career, he took up several creative writing courses in Canada and the United States. He had no idea it would have taken him ten long years of hard work and dedication to bring his creative writing to life. He really wanted to entertain his audience, and to make them feel they were part of the story, and without an audience, there would be no story to tell.

Creative writing has changed Frank Senauth throughout the years, as he has learnt to write for an audience rather than for himself. After many years of developing his pose, he felt ready to take on the world with his fascinating writing. His first novel was, "A Wish to Die – A Will to Live', which was published in the United Kingdom in October 1997. The author hopes you'll enjoy reading his work as he enjoyed writing it.

Senauth's last book was, `The Making of Jamaica' which was published by AuthorHouse in the United States of America in 2011

CPSIA information can be obtained at www.ICGtesting.com
Printed in the USA
LVOW121833280212

270827LV00026B/173/P